ADVANCE PRAISE FOR
Life and Other Shortcomings

"All that glitters is not gold in Corie Adjmi's wonderful short story collection *Life and Other Shortcomings*. Adjmi exposes the fear, envy, and yearning that simmer just beneath the surface of her characters' beautiful lives. Her writing is both elegant and powerful. I was hooked from the first page to the last."
—Ellen Sussman, *New York Times* best-selling author of four novels, *A Wedding in Provence*, *The Paradise Guest House*, *French Lessons* and *On a Night Like This*

"Corie Adjmi's stories are sharply written, unsparing, and spot-on. With wisdom and humanity, *Life and Other Shortcomings* plumbs the mysteries of adult life: the menacing underside of love, the protean nature of grief, and the baffling difficulty of staying true to ourselves and the things we value most. Assured in her storytelling, Adjmi writes with force and perception. Her stories are a must-read."
—Elyssa Friedland, author of *The Floating Feldmans* and *The Intermission and Love and Miss Communication*

"Pitch perfect and very haunting, *Life and Other Shortcomings* is a true delight. Adjmi's interlocking stories are as funny as they are tragic. Her characters are so real and relatable, you'll find yourself rooting for them, even as they get into trouble. Adjmi is a great new talent."
—Alison Espach, author of *The Adults*

"Corie Adjmi has a flair for dramati~'
in on the killer moment, and her dia.
was cringing at times . . . It is just so
—Susan Breen, auth

LIFE

AND

OTHER

SHORTCOMINGS

LIFE

AND

OTHER

SHORTCOMINGS

❦ STORIES ❧

CORIE ADJMI

SHE WRITES PRESS

Published 2020
Printed in the United States of America
ISBN: 978-1-63152-713-5 pbk
ISBN: 978-1-63152-714-2 ebk
Library of Congress Control Number: 2020904538

For information, address:
She Writes Press
1569 Solano Ave #546
Berkeley, CA 94707

She Writes Press is a division of SparkPoint Studio, LLC.

Book design by Stacey Aaronson

Versions of these stories have previously appeared elsewhere: "Dinner Conversation" in *Licking River Review* and *Crucible*; "The Devil Makes Three" in *Whetstone* and *Red Rock Review*; "Blind Man's Bluff" in *South Dakota Review*; "Sunny Side Up" in *Green Hills Literary Lantern*; "The Joker" in *Indiana Review*; "Happily Ever After" in *RiverSedge*; "Lucky" in RE:AL; "Shadows and Partially Lit Faces" in *Pangolin Papers*; "All You Touch" in *Diverse Voices Quarterly*; "That's How It Was With Howie" in *Diverse Voices Quarterly*, *TheTalonMag*, and *Verdad*; and "Tick Tock" in *Crack the Spine*.

CONTENTS

ℰ DINNER CONVERSATION

We sit three couples as we always do, boy girl, boy girl, with no married couples next to each other. When we were first married, I didn't like this. Now I don't care.

It is 1998, and this New York City restaurant just recently opened. It's a happening kind of place populated by the cool and the young—part bar, part restaurant, part lounge. Red walls make you feel both sexy and regal. Music beats in the background. It's the kind that seeps into your skin and pulses under your bones.

We sit at a large round table and a waitress, her hair tied back in a ponytail, approaches us. She isn't wearing any makeup, and she exudes a wholesome sexuality that, I have to admit, is alluring. She hands each of us a menu and lights a candle in the center of the table. She moves like an exotic bird, graceful and deliberate. I have just laid eyes on this woman, and already I am threatened by her natural beauty and her presence. She stands beside me, both feet grounded.

I play a game. I spot a person, and based on how they look, what they wear, and how they stand, I draw up a whole life for them: if they're married or not, where they live, what their apartment or house looks like, and what they do for a living. I decide that she's an aspiring actress, living in an apartment in the Village, venturing toward her dream.

Marisa, a Monica Lewinsky look-alike, sits to the right of my husband, Dylan. They went to high school together, and, when she married Eric, Dylan marched in their wedding. When Dylan and I started dating, he wanted me to get to know them. He didn't care what his mother thought about me; he wanted Marisa to like me. And she did.

Dana, who is tall and blonde, sits to Dylan's left. She just got back from a spa in California and she's lost weight. She looks too skinny to me—the bones in her wrist protrude like large marbles. But who am I to judge? Dylan says you can never be too skinny; it's like being too rich.

I watch my husband as he entertains. I pay special attention as he leans in to say something to Dana. She throws her head back and laughs.

Dylan and I have been friends with Dana and Peter for close to fifteen years. We met them at a parenting class we took before the birth of our first child. Dylan was complaining about having to be there on a Monday night during football season, and Peter overheard him. They took off early and went to a bar across the street to watch the end of the game.

We've all been friends ever since. We know this is unusual. About ten years ago, five years into the friendship, five years' worth of dinners and vacations and cocktail parties, we named ourselves: we are "The Sixers."

When the waitress returns, she places a basket of bread on our table. Marisa, who is facing the wall, turns her body dramatically, her long black hair swinging over her shoulder. It isn't often that Marisa doesn't sit facing out, able to see the crowd, and she wants everyone at our table to notice her strain.

"What can I get you?" the waitress asks.

I know what Dylan is thinking. He gets that look on his face, the one I recognize all too well. The one he, at one time, reserved for me. His eyes glimmer like two perfect diamonds. "What's your name?" he asks the waitress.

"Judy," she says, smiling, her teeth lined up like a row of miniature marshmallows.

"Hi, Judy," Dylan flirts. "Nice to meet you. We'll have two bottles of Pellegrino for the table, and I'll have a Glenrothes, neat."

Judy takes our drink order, and Dylan looks at me. "You're going to eat that?"

I slip the breadstick out of my mouth and scan the table to see who has heard this. I've gained weight, and it bothers Dylan that his wife is getting fat. I'm not sure how I feel about it. At first it was a surprise, but now I kind of like the extra weight. It makes me feel stronger, more grounded. But Dylan has no patience for fat. Fat, in his view, is a complete betrayal of a body, and it represents a person without discipline or self-respect. Pregnancy is no exception. And while I felt full and complete, voluptuous, and even beautiful as I carried my three children to term, I knew that Dylan couldn't look at me.

After I gave birth to David, our first, just a week after his bris, Dylan replaced the whole milk with skim, and every product in our cabinet said fat free. I suppose he wanted back the wife he'd married, but I could no longer play that part.

I glance at Eric, who is sitting to my right. He told me I looked beautiful during my last pregnancy. You have to love a guy who thinks a pregnant woman is beautiful. Dylan professes that a man who compliments a pregnant woman is blind, stupid, or simply playing his cards right, knowing that this is a temporary condition, and that in a matter of months the woman will give birth, remember the compliment, and be forever grateful.

"I have a question," I say, reaching for my glass of red wine. "If you had a flaw, something that bothered you about yourself, like a really big nose, a bald spot, or one eyebrow, would you do something to fix it?" I bring the glass to my lips and take a sip, glancing at my friends over the rim.

"Well, it depends what you're talking about exactly," Peter says. He covers one eyebrow with a hand like a patch and says, "I mean I couldn't very well walk around like this."

"Not like that," I giggle, and I glide my finger across my forehead, demonstrating. "I mean a unibrow. You know, one big brow. No space in between." Doubled over, I laugh some more. The sound emerges from inside me uncontrollably. This has happened before, the giving of myself so completely that I know if I don't concentrate, I could pee.

I've taken to asking questions like this lately. My friends like it. "On a scale of one to ten," I ask, "what do you give her?" I point to a tall blonde at the table next to us. Or I might ask, "If you were stuck on a desert island with one person, and you were going to have to live with that person alone forever, who would you absolutely never sleep with? Even if it meant no sex forever."

We all work to entertain each other like television. Last month at a party, we played the Newlywed Game. Our questions ranged from dull to spectacular: from "What color is your spouse's toothbrush?" to "What's your favorite part of your spouse's body?" and finally, "If your sex life is candy, would you describe it as a Zero Bar, Fun Dip, a Blow Pop, or a Marathon Bar?"

Occasionally I like it. But there's a line somewhere, a boundary that we cross sometimes, not knowing it until it's too late. And then it's simply too late, and you can't go back.

A cell phone rings, and Dylan reaches for his most recent toy. "Hello," he says, getting up from the table. As he strolls away, mouthing "Excuse me," I watch him walk and I'm still taken by his good looks. Sometimes I stand back and observe him objectively, as if he isn't mine. And I see what other women see, and I remember how I felt the first time I met him. It was at a party. I spotted him from across the room. Every girl there wanted to know who he was. And so when he strutted over to me, picked me out of everyone there, I was completely flattered. I felt like a child who'd just won a prize at a carnival and thought that if I didn't lean on something, I'd fall.

Studying how he was dressed, I imagined him to be a successful businessman living in Manhattan. I was right. Charmed, I listened intently as he told me about his travels to Europe. But what really got me, what drew me in, was that he'd just returned from a rafting trip in Chile where he'd camped out, pitched his own tent, hiked, and mountain climbed. He was a doer, and I liked that. He didn't sit around watching life go by; he lived it. I was completely attracted to him, and I stepped in closer as he talked. Without my consent, my hips swayed to the music, and it became difficult to speak through my continuous smile.

Dylan fed me a line. "You're quite special," he said. "Sexy, too."

And from that point I focused on what I believed he'd want to hear. In doing that, I ignored or simply covered up parts of myself. And like water under oil, what was on the bottom had no chance to surface.

When Dylan returns to the table, he says, "Sorry about that."

Peter squints, extending his arms as he holds his menu.

"What's the matter, Peter? Need longer arms?" Dylan asks.

"This is ludicrous. Look how small the print is. Who could see this?"

"I can see it fine, honey," Dana says, leaning forward, her black turtleneck sweater accentuating her Ivory-girl skin. "Maybe it's time for you to get those glasses?"

"No way," Peter glares at the menu. "I can see." He leans over to me and, pointing, whispers, "What does this say?"

The waitress returns. "What can I get you?" Her confidence is captivating. I stare at her as if by observing closely I could inhabit that sureness.

"Well, I think I'd like the cod," Marisa says as she looks up at her. "Is it good?"

"Yes. It's very good."

"But can I get it without the sauce?" She tilts her head.

The waitress smiles and says, "You want it plain?"

"Yes. Can I have it grilled?"

"That shouldn't be a problem."

"Do you think I can get spinach instead of eggplant?"

The waitress looks behind her as if needing to be rescued, then says, "I'll have to ask the chef about that."

Marisa doesn't care that she's annoying the waitress. She feels entitled to what she wants, and she never stops until she gets it. Calculating the end, she justifies the means. Like the time at Disney World when she paid a man at the front of the admission line to switch spots with her. She wasn't about to wait an hour on line just to pay, but she didn't want to disappoint her kids. In her mind, all was fair, and she was proud of what she considered a clever idea. She rationalized that she didn't cut the line, the man she'd switched places with was happy with his extra fifty bucks, and her kids didn't have to wait. Something about it rubbed me the wrong way. Something about it wasn't right, but I couldn't put my finger on it.

"Oh, and can I get a salad instead of mashed potatoes?" Marisa says.

Eric winks at the waitress and says, "Judy, she'll have an Absolut martini but instead of olives, can she get the salmon appetizer?"

"Very funny," Marisa says, throwing Eric a look.

"I'll work it out," the waitress says.

When I told my friend, Willow, how we call ourselves the Sixers, she laughed, reinforcing the idea that we should have our own television series. I played into this and told her about the time we took a boat out for the day and named ourselves after the characters on *Gilligan's Island*. It was easy. I was Mary Ann, of course. Down-to-earth, brown hair, and sneakers. Dana was Ginger, and she loved that. Glamorous and famous. Dana and I snickered, thinking Marisa wouldn't want to be Mrs. Howell, old and fussy, but she surprised us both, thrilled with the idea of being her, yearning to be doted over and determined to be filthy rich. Eric now calls her "Lovey," and she has taken this persona to a whole new level. Initially craving caviar and diamonds, she now claims to identify with the French. She has gone from being a New York housewife to a European princess. There is irony in the fact that we have relegated ourselves to being nothing more than characters in a sitcom.

Dylan asks Dana, "How's your salad?"

"It's great." She moves the goat cheese to the far corners of her plate.

I eat spaghetti with a mushroom cream sauce, each bite filling me like earth in a giant hole. I look up and see Dylan watching me.

"Do you think it matters if your spouse puts on some weight?" I ask. "Peter, are you more attracted to Dana because she's thin?"

"Yes."

"Yes?"

"Yeah. I mean, I'd love her either way. But you know, when we're in bed," he pierces a tomato with his fork, "I like to be able to flip her around a bit. Couldn't do that with extra weight aboard."

"Men are pigs," Marisa says.

I twist spaghetti around my fork. "It's our own fault. We buy into it."

Dylan is looking at me. He raises one finger to his mouth and gives me the signal we came up with years ago, a warning that there is something in my teeth. I work at the space between my two front teeth, and he indicates I should move to the left.

Dana leans in and speaks in her usual soft-spoken, almost hushed manner. "I know a woman who sets her alarm for six o'clock every morning so she can put on a full face of makeup before her husband wakes up. And at night, she waits for him to fall asleep before she takes it off."

"Sounds like my kind of woman," Dylan says.

"Recently Dylan told me that when I lie down, my breasts are messy. Can you please explain that? What does that mean?" I wipe cream sauce from my mouth as if it were just as easy to wipe away the hurt. I'm not embarrassed to repeat this. I like my breasts, and in revealing what Dylan said to me, I'm attempting to expose him for the jerk he can be. I look around the table searching for a reaction, but this statement comes off as matter-of-factly as if I were reporting the weather.

"It means he wants you to get implants," Marisa says. "Then they'll be hard and unmoving, never messy or out of place."

Sometimes, I must admit, I love how Marisa articulates what's on her mind, remarks on how things are, whether we like it or not.

"I told Peter," Dana says, "that I love him the way he is, and that even though he is miserable about losing his hair, I think he shouldn't do a thing. He wants to have a hair transplant."

"If you want hair, of course you should have a transplant," Dylan says, placing a forkful of tuna appetizer into his mouth.

"That's easy for you to say," Peter snorts, knocking on the table. "Your head is like wood. You have no feeling."

We all laugh. Dylan leans over and whispers something to Marisa.

"What are you two whispering about? Are you talking about me?" Dana asks.

"You are unbelievable," Peter says. "You always think everything's about you."

This statement shoots across the table like a dart,

landing in Dana's heart, and I can see pain on her face. I figured it out recently. A spouse blurts close to twenty of these comments each day. Simple things, really. Questions like, "You're wearing that?" Or "Why'd you buy the big one?" But they add up. They accumulate, and twenty comments a day equals one hundred and forty darts each week, five hundred and sixty per month.

A busboy comes to clear the table, and he gathers our plates, stacking them like the mozzarella, eggplant, and red pepper tower Eric ate.

"He is the smallest person I've ever seen," Dylan says. "I wonder if they pay him by the inch."

I glance around the table. Everyone is laughing. I don't think it's funny at all. I think it's mean.

"Excuse me," I say, standing and pushing my chair in.

In the bathroom I look at myself in the mirror, wondering when I began this double life; two lives coexisting side by side like twins in a womb. In actuality, I've learned to lie, sparing others and hurting myself. When it starts, it's the small things, like when you're dying for moo goo gai pan, craving it so bad you can taste it, and you hear yourself say, "I don't care, Chinese or Mexican, either one is fine with me." But it gets worse, all your feelings lost, numbness growing like bacteria slowly destroying you until you are unable to recognize if you are hot or cold, tired or hungry, miserable or happy. I reach for soap and allow my hands to linger under the water.

The bathroom door opens, and Dana comes in. She stops to look at herself in the mirror, and then she opens her purse and pulls out a brush, lip gloss, and lip liner.

"Prescriptives," she says, "the best," as she outlines her lips. "Want to use it?"

"No, thanks. I have my own." I dig in my purse.

"Don't do that."

I look up. "What?"

"You're squinting."

"Oh. I didn't realize."

Dana brushes her long blonde hair. "You do that a lot."

"Do what?"

"Squint. I mean, you move your face a lot when you talk."

"That's called expression, Dana."

"Yeah, but it's not worth it. You have to live with that skin for the rest of your life. You should be more careful."

I realize I am having this conversation with a reflection in the bathroom mirror. And I remind myself that while Dana has her flaws, she's a good person. She'd do anything for me.

Back at the table Eric is saying, in a somewhat British accent even though he was born and raised in Brooklyn, how he and Marisa had gone to Barneys together that day and bought a fabulous set of dishes.

When I'd just given birth to David and was not able to leave him, Dylan wanted me to hire a baby nurse so I could go out for dinner and travel. He said if I stopped breastfeeding I'd lose weight faster. As if to prove a point or punish me, one Sunday he went antique shopping without me and returned at the end of the day with a slew of collectibles for our brand-new bookcase. I told him that I wanted to gather things for the shelves together slowly, over the years. Objects, books, and photographs of the moments of our lives. Dylan acted as if he didn't hear me, my voice trailing off, fleeting like an echo, until it eventually disappeared, unheard, as if unspoken, while he continued to pull collections of books from the boxes. On the coffee table he piled a pair of gold binoculars, an artifact from a ship, two brown leather satchels, and vases. I tried again to explain to him that I wanted each item on our bookcase to have personal meaning, that our books should be ones we had actually read. But Dylan needed the shelves full, and he needed them to look a certain way, neat and uniform—identical leather spines evenly lined up.

It wasn't until he flipped through one of the last books that he understood what I was trying to say. The title page read, *The Life and Times of Jesus Christ.* We're Jewish, and it wasn't the kind of thing he would ever read. But because Dylan could never be completely wrong, we decided to keep some of the items: one satchel, a vase, and the gold binoculars. Everything else went back the next day. "This wouldn't have happened if you'd come with me," Dylan said.

When the main course arrives, Marisa says, "I know something that I'm not supposed to know." She looks around, making sure she has everyone's attention.

"What do you know?" Dana asks, cutting into a grilled portabella mushroom as if it were a steak.

Marisa leans in and casts her eyes downward, one shoulder forward so that her button-down silk shirt opens, revealing a purple lace bra. My eyes fasten on it, and I think that lace is an interesting invention. A fabric with holes, a tapestry you can see through, and yet it obscures.

"I really shouldn't tell." She brings her other shoulder forward.

"Oh, that's not right. You can't say something like that

and then not finish. You just can't do that," Dana says, as if reciting the rules to a game.

"Well, did you notice Lori was at the Murphys' party by herself? She told everyone that Howie was out of town." Marisa turns her head from side to side. "I heard he was in town. Didn't go to the party because they're separated. She's moved out, and she's living in an apartment in the city."

"Why?" I ask. "They seemed like such a nice couple."

"That's what they wanted everyone to think," Marisa says.

"Just last week I was complaining to Peter that he should be more like Howie. You know, more affectionate." Dana dabs her lips with her napkin.

"You never know what goes on behind closed doors," Marisa says.

Dylan speaks but doesn't focus on anyone in particular. "There should be a renewal policy on marriage. Like a lease. Every two years you can renegotiate. Renew, or not."

"I like that," Peter says, extending his arm as if he were to shake on it. "That'll keep 'em on their toes." He takes a bite of his poached salmon.

"Who's them?" Dana asks.

"Women, my love." Chewing, Peter continues, "After all, marriage is a ridiculous concept, created for one purpose."

"And what's that?" Marisa asks.

"For women to have economic security," he says, swallowing.

Eric dips his napkin into a glass of water and rubs at the stain on his shirt. "People used to get married at fifteen and die at thirty. They were together for fifteen years. Today if you get married at twenty-five, and live to seventy-five, you could theoretically be married for fifty years."

Marisa winks at him. "Lucky you."

"What a shame," I say. "All those years. And their daughter, Olivia. How is Olivia?"

"I hear it's been really hard on her," Marisa answers.

"Can we change the subject, please?" Peter says. "This is bringing my head down."

"I agree," Dana says. "Let's move on." She pushes up her sleeves and lifts her drink. "What'd you do today, Callie?"

"I spent the day with Kelly. We had lunch and then went to the Met."

"Now that sounds interesting," Peter says, reaching for his drink.

"What?"

"You and Kelly."

"What are you talking about, Peter?"

"Come on, Callie, you know what they say about Kelly."

"No, I don't, Peter. What do they say about Kelly?"

Peter rotates his wrist, spinning ice around in his glass. "They say"—he places his glass down on the table—"she likes girls."

"Why, why do people say that? Because she's not married?" I dip bread in olive oil. "That doesn't mean anything, Peter, and anyway, I'm not interested."

Peter looks into my eyes. "Oh, come on. Not even a little?"

I swallow. "Not even a little."

"You're in denial, Callie." He leans back and clasps his hands on his crossed legs. "All bottled up." He drags this out.

"Can't I have my own preferences and desires without you telling me what I want?"

Dylan looks at Peter and chuckles. "Maybe you can tell *me* what she wants."

"What if I don't believe you know what you want?" Peter continues.

"And you know what I want?" I ask.

"Maybe I do," he says. "Look, Callie, don't take it so personally. Most people don't know what they want."

"So that means," I say, "you could be interested in Dylan?"

"Yes, it means that."

Dylan bats his eyelashes, "Peter, I didn't know."

"Oh my God." I shake my head.

"Peter!" Dana throws her crumpled napkin at him from across the table. "What are you saying?" This is as loud as I've ever heard Dana speak.

"So, what *are* you saying, Peter?" I lift my glass, and, while I'm interested in his answer, I'm momentarily distracted by the impression my lipstick has left behind on the rim. I use my napkin to wipe it and turn to look at him. My hair falls in front of my face, a shield.

"I'm saying that everyone is everything." He stabs a roasted potato and sticks it in his mouth. "Capable of anything, if you allow yourself."

"Oh, really," I say, shaking my head. "So, I personally could be a woman walking in the countryside, a woman at work in New York City, a mom, a hooker, and a lesbian?"

"Exactly."

"Are you saying we could be any of them?"

Peter brings the glass of scotch to his lips. "I'm saying you could be all of them."

"So, we pick which parts we'll act? Like in a play?"

"Something like that."

Dana leans in. "It's about . . ."

"Choice," Peter finishes.

I shake my head. "Homosexuality is not necessarily a choice."

"No," Peter says. "But not acting on one's homosexuality might be."

I think about this. How much of myself, I wonder, is an act?

Earlier that morning, I picked up Dylan's wet towel from our bedroom floor and closed his closet doors. In the bathroom, I wiped off the toothpaste he left on the side of the sink, bent for his boxer shorts, and dropped them in the hamper. Dylan slinked up behind me and reached for my hair clip, snapping it off. The act, like the plucking of feathers from a chicken, felt as if he were snatchng a part of me.

"Do you wear hair clips?" I ask the women at the table, and realize that I have never seen any of them wearing one.

"No way," Marisa answers. "Eric hates my hair up."

"What about when you're working in your house—cooking, gardening, or cleaning?"

"I'll wear a ponytail sometimes, but never a clip," Marisa informs me.

"Women who walk around like that look like house-keepers," Dana says.

I bring the glass of wine that the waitress, Judy, has just set down on the table to my lips. "What if you're actually keeping house?"

Dana scoops an olive out of her drink and says, "My

father once threw a woman wearing curlers out of his office. Wouldn't examine her with rollers in her hair. When she explained to my father that she had somewhere to go later on, he told her that she was already somewhere and that she shouldn't walk around that way. According to him, it was unacceptable."

Dana sits straight up with her shoulders pinned to the back of her chair. I watch her lips moving as she rolls the olive around in her mouth. Using two fingers, she removes the pit and says, "It's like wearing flats—you just don't."

"But Dana, you're five-foot-nine," I say.

"You just don't, Callie. Look at your legs in heels, and then look at them in a pair of flats."

I'm not sure how to respond to this, so I don't.

I think about the year before when I traveled to a spa in California, a man with messy hair and sunglasses wanted to know my name. I told him, and the next day, he asked me again. By that afternoon, he'd asked me my name four separate times.

"Why do you keep asking me that?" I said to him. "If you're trying to flirt with me it would be a much better tactic if you could remember my name."

He looked at me sincerely. "It's just that when you say your name"—he lifted his sunglasses from his nose —"it's like you don't believe it."

"Let's play a game," Marisa says.

"What kind of game?" Dylan asks.

"Each one of us has to use three words to describe ourselves." She looks around. "Callie, you go first."

Thoughts spin around in my head like clothes in a dryer. The colors and fabrics collide and separate. Should

I reveal what I really think about myself, or should I tell them what I wish to be? I feel unnaturally troubled, like a turtle burdened by the weight of its own shell. I reach for dessert, as if this is the same as reaching for the truth, and in a moment of madness, an attempt at honesty, I think to say, flawed, secretive, and angry.

Instead, I take a bite of tiramisu, the white cream resting on my top lip, and the words emerge from inside me.

"Good, honest, and open," I say.

I stick my tongue out of my mouth and lick the white cream off.

ᴄᴜ SUNNY SIDE UP

T he day my family moved from an apartment on Robert
E. Lee Street to a house on Canal Boulevard, it was
boiling out. It was the fall of 1970. I was six, and my
mother was eight months pregnant. While my father got
ready for work, my mother lugged a box of shoes to the
door, and by the look on her face, I knew something was
wrong. She pushed back her thick, yellow headband and
wiped her forehead. "It's unbearable," she said. She stood
and lifted her arms, exposing her belly under her mater-
nity blouse, held her long black hair with one hand, and
fanned the back of her neck with the other. "You could fry
an egg on the sidewalk in this city."

My father reached for his watch and fastened it around
his wrist. "You mean it's hot. Can't you just say it's hot?"

"You can say it's hot." She bent and taped the box
shut. "I want to say, you can fry an egg on the sidewalk."
My mother hated New Orleans and wanted desperately
to move back to New York, and I could feel her nerves.

"After all," she said, standing, "to each his own."

"What do you want from me, Sharon? I don't control
the weather."

"I didn't say you did."

Sometimes when I close my eyes, I see myself small
and alone at the window watching my father walk away
that day. I vividly remember wanting to go with him.

His leaving triggered something in my mother. She seemed distracted and teary-eyed. "What's wrong?" I asked.

She inhaled deeply and transformed herself from a twenty-four-year-old into a full-fledged adult. "Nothing," she said, wiping her eyes. "What could be wrong? Daddy went to work, and we get to move into our beautiful new house." Busying herself immediately, she packed away her feelings along with her belongings. She placed her jewelry in a black velvet pouch, secured the pouch in her bra, and slammed the door to our apartment shut.

We followed the moving truck to our new house in our black Cadillac, the seats the color of red licorice. My mother thought black seats were classier, but my father got the red anyway.

"I can't believe we're doing this," my mother mumbled. She turned a corner, and there was dead silence.

Our new house was an orange brick ranch. There was a pool in the backyard and a magnolia tree in the front. Unwilling to accommodate themselves to the grass, the tree's roots radiated in all directions, sprawling under the concrete, strong enough to lift a slab of the driveway. My father had taken me to see the tree the week before we moved. "This is the most special tree in all of New Orleans," he'd said. He hoisted me up, and I sat on his shoulders with my head amongst the leaves, imagining each broad leaf as a magic carpet.

My mother didn't care about the tree the way my father did. She paraded right past it, unlocked the front door, marched through the living room, and stomped straight to the hallway. She flicked a switch, and we heard a humming sound. "It'll cool off in here in no time," she said.

I stood against the living room wall as she'd instructed and watched as two moving men fumbled like out of sync dance partners with our yellow velvet couch. It wasn't long before the wall-to-wall green carpet was littered with boxes piled three high, and I pretended to be trapped by the barricade.

My mother bent to lift a box, but as she stood she let out a groan and cradled her pregnant stomach.

"Hold on," one of the movers said. "Let me do that." He looped his bare arm around her and led her to the couch. "You shouldn't be carrying those heavy boxes."

In spite of herself, my mother sighed as she sat. It wasn't like her to show vulnerability, especially to a man.

Sweat dripped from the mover's cap. He wiped his face with his shirt, and I studied his flexed arm, noticing that he was bigger than my father. He headed for his truck and returned with a thermos and two Dixie cups. He poured water from the thermos into the two cups and handed one to my mother. "Here. Drink this," he said. He handed me a cup too. His fingers were rough, as if covered with dried glue.

"I'm fine," my mother insisted. "Thank you for your concern." She stood and began to unpack. "Look at this mess," she said. "We'll never get this place organized."

My mother insisted it was a virtue to be methodical, and she extended this belief to every aspect of her life. In her desk drawer she kept a stapler, a pad of paper, and a pen. These items were always in the same place. My mother paid bills at that desk the way men serve in the army with honor and pride. She never paid late, and she called this her work. "How do you think soap gets into this house? It doesn't just fly into the cabinet alongside the toothpaste and deodorant. And," she continued, "did you ever, ever go to get toilet paper and there wasn't any? Never," she answered herself.

She opened the box I had drawn a smiley face on. "We'll start unpacking in your room," she said. The room had three windows, which allowed the sun great access, and the bed was queen-size. "For a queen," my mother said. I stood on one side, she on the other, and we pulled the sheet tightly over the mattress.

Alphabetically, my mother lined up items in her medicine cabinet: Bayer, Colgate, Ponds, Right Guard, Q-tips, Tylenol.

"We shouldn't have to do this alone," she said. "Your father should be here. Can't count on Aunt Susie, she's busy with her own life. Ultimately," she continued, "you have to depend on yourself. Can't count on anybody else."

My mother tried to mask her desperation, but sometimes her loneliness got the best of her. Swept up by my father's charm, she married him at seventeen and was surprised to learn, six months into their marriage, that he wanted to move to New Orleans and open up an antiques store in the French Quarter more than he wanted to stay in New York and work with her father in his wholesale business as originally planned. Nine months later I came along.

"You're a good girl, Callie," she said. "And don't think I don't appreciate it, because I do." She handed me a box of saltines and a couple of Oreos. "You're the only thing keeping me sane."

Recently, my mother confessed she didn't have the slightest idea what to do with me when I was born. So she hired a nurse—an old black woman named Jenny. My mother claimed Jenny took care of me better than she could, like a mother who gives up a child for adoption, insisting that the adoptive mother could do a better job. Jenny fed me, changed me, and sang to me for the first month of my life. And then, on the thirtieth day, because she had another job, she packed her bags and left.

"Your father warned me," my mother chuckled. "He told me to practice taking care of you while Jenny was still there. But I couldn't. When Jenny walked out, I wanted to walk out with her. I took a good look at you. 'It's you and me, kid,' I said. I pulled you in close and cried."

I imagined that moment—me pressed against her, our bodies resting on one another, moving like a river—and felt sad knowing those moments didn't come often. It was as if my mother had missed hearing the rules to a game and then was forced to play.

Morning dragged on. I wished my father would come home. I wanted him to laugh with my mother and me like he did the last time the three of us played Monkey in the Middle. When my father was in the middle, he jumped up and down like a gorilla and scratched under his arms. When it was my mother's turn to be in the middle, my father instructed me to throw the ball high. "She hasn't got a shot," he snickered. "She can't jump with that belly." My mother lasted five minutes before she excused herself, saying that this was no game for a big, fat pregnant lady.

"OK, you can quit if you want to," my father said. "But then I win." He strutted between her and me like a dancer on *Soul Train*. My mother laughed, and my father winked at her. "Would you like to dance?" he asked her in a fake English accent.

"I'd be delighted," she said. And they danced the way

couples do on their wedding night. For years, every time I thought of my childhood, I retrieved moments like this one, memories playing out like a fairy tale, one contrived scene after another. Because I so desperately wanted my parents to be happy, I developed a knack, an uncanny ability to deny and shut out any evidence that was contrary.

By late afternoon I was going crazy with boredom watching my mother unpack everything from our Shabbat candlesticks to my father's underwear, but I knew better than to complain. I reached inside a box and fished out a teacup and saucer painted with red roses, and then I sat down for some imaginary tea. I extended my pinky and took a sip.

My mother came up behind me. "Callie!" she yelled. "Don't touch that." I jumped, and the teacup fell from my hand. It clanked on the saucer, and the handle broke off. "Now look what you've done," she screamed, and even though my mother was only five foot one, she towered over me, full of rage, gigantic. I stayed out of her way for the rest of the day.

It was six o'clock when we heard my father sing, "I'm home."

My mother crammed the last few albums into her Louis XIV armoire and mumbled, "It's about time."

I ran to my father and jumped into his arms, hooking my legs behind him. He spun around.

"I'm getting dizzy, Daddy. Stop it," I squealed. This was the most fun I'd had all day.

My mother carried in an empty box. "Oh, you decided to join us."

"Yep," he said. He kissed her on the cheek, looked over her shoulder, and asked, "What's for dinner?"

"Very funny."

"What do you mean?"

"How could I possibly make dinner? Look at this place."

"Sharon, I had a hard day. I'm hungry."

My father put me down, and I sat on the floor in between them, still dizzy from the spinning.

"I've only got two hands, Steven. I've been here all day by myself. I'm pregnant and tired."

I wished I could disappear. My father was easygoing about some things. He was even going to let my mother decorate their new bedroom pink. But food wasn't something he was laid-back about. "Damn it, Sharon." He slammed his hand on the Formica counter. "Do I ever tell you I can't give you money? I do my part; why can't you do yours?" He charged out, and the screen door slammed behind him.

I followed him outside. He unlatched the gate to the pool, and we stood near the edge of it. Our reflections trembled above the water. The sun slanted down on us, the air thick. Neither one of us said a word. A mosquito buzzed between us and then landed on my father's cheek. He swatted at it, and it flew away. Across the pool there was a blue light. The mosquito landed on it and, with a loud zap, fell into a pile of dead bugs.

"That's so mean," I said.

"Would you rather they bite you?"

I was struck by his question. My father knew how to take care of himself, but as a girl, I was already learning to accommodate, and the answer was not clear.

Often when my father was upset, I took it upon myself to make him happy again. Sometimes if I climbed on his lap and hugged him, he'd momentarily snap out of his sadness, appreciating my love, but he'd often return from these moments as forlorn as he'd started. I reached for his hand.

"Come on," he said. "Let's go pick up some Chicken Delight."

AT the restaurant there was a hand-painted rooster on the wall behind the counter. Each feather was carefully delineated, and it made the chicken look real. I've always hated thinking about food as the animal it once was, but it seemed that people wanted to be reminded that the food they ate was not artificial, canned, or frozen.

"They want it fresh, and they want it fast," my father said.

"Yuck."

"That's why everyone loves Manales. They get to pick the exact lobster they want from the tank. Then it's boiled right on the spot."

"That's disgusting."

He made his hands into a gun and aimed at the chicken behind the counter. "You're right," he said, laughing. "It's murder with intent."

"What can I get you?" the girl behind the counter asked. She wore a chef's hat with a chicken on the front.

My father smirked. "You really want to know?

She put her pad down. "Excuse me?"

My father turned his back to me, leaning in to her, but I could still hear. "I like your shirt," he said, pointing to the bow.

My father was handsome, and he liked that women

found him attractive. He did what he could to maintain his good looks, buying fancy shirts and wearing them with two or three buttons undone. Every Saturday for years, I sat on his feet while he did one hundred sit-ups. Then he'd stand in his bikini underwear, pat his stomach while sucking it in, and say, "Not bad, huh?" After, he'd hit the floor again and do fifty push-ups.

A boy plunged a bin of fries into hot oil and steam billowed behind the girl. My father ordered a bucket of fried chicken, coleslaw, and potato salad.

"This is for you," the girl behind the counter said, handing me a chicken hat like the one she wore and a plastic egg with a chick inside. She shrugged. "It's free when you buy a bucket."

We drove home with the windows down. The air outside was warm, the sun low on the horizon. My father turned on the radio and sang "Satisfaction." He poked at my ribs with one finger, then lifted his arms. "Look, no hands." The car swerved, and I grabbed hold of the handle on the door.

"Daddy, stop."

He veered back and forth over the painted white line on the road, making our journey home as exhilarating as the roller coaster ride at Pontchartrain Beach. "Look, I can do this with my eyes closed."

"Daddy, open your eyes."

"Don't you trust me?" he asked. "You think you could do a better job? Come on, let's see." He patted his thighs.

I climbed on his lap, thrilled to be part of the excitement. I gripped the steering wheel, and he rested his hands on mine. He let me come unreasonably close to hitting a tree before he took control of the wheel.

"Watch where you're going." He laughed.

When he'd had enough, he told me to go back to my seat. He stared straight ahead and seemed to be in his own world, far away from me. That's how it was with my father. Sometimes he was right there next to you, and then, *poof*, he was gone.

Then he looked at me and said, as if this was the most important advice he could ever give, "You only live once." He stepped on the gas, and I fell back against the seat.

"You're going too fast, Daddy."

A dog darted into the road. He slammed on the brakes, and I hit the dashboard with a thud. Blood streamed from my mouth. I touched my lips and found my fingers red. As I cried, my father rocked me in his arms. He leaned to open the glove compartment, which was no longer ordered the way my mother usually left it: tissues on the left and car manuals evenly lined up on the right. He grabbed a handful of tissues and blotted my lips. "Hold this," he said. He glanced at the bucket of toppled chicken and picked up the pieces. "Your mother's going to kill me," he said, sweeping up the crumbs. He reorganized the glove compartment. "You OK?"

I took a deep breath. "I just want to go home," I said.

MY mother gave my father a chilling look when she saw my bloody mouth.

"What?" my father threw his arms up in disbelief. "What are you looking at?"

"Nothing," my mother said, turning from him.

"It was an accident, Sharon."

She grabbed a dishtowel and scrubbed at the bloodstain on my white dress. Then she plucked carpet hairs from the chicken and arranged the pieces on a platter as if she'd cooked it herself.

While we ate, my father tried once or twice to engage my mother in conversation, but she stayed slumped in her chair and refused to look at him. The quiet was killing me.

I reached for my Coke but drank from the straw too fast, and I choked.

My father leaned in.

I coughed louder.

"Lift your arms," my mother said.

I raised my arms above my head but kept coughing. She reached over and patted my back, but I couldn't catch my breath. "She's really choking, Steven."

My father shot out of his chair and stood next to me. "Is it a bone? What is it?"

Just as I began to catch my breath, I saw my parents standing side by side, positioned like a team in front of me. Instead of telling them I was fine, I held my breath and threw my hands around my neck. My mother panicked, full of fear, and her eyes linked with my father's.

"She's blue, Steven. Do something."

"Get water," he ordered, and he yanked me from my chair. He held my arms over my head with one hand and smacked my back with his other. My mother returned with water, and my father held the glass for me while I drank. I took a breath.

"Thank God," my mother said.

My father hugged me and insisted I sit on his lap for the rest of dinner. I asked if he would play airplane and, overjoyed, he circled his spoon above my head, made engine noises, and landed every bite safely in my mouth. My mother was too nervous to sit still, so she stacked plates and cleared the table. "Never a dull moment," she said.

After dinner she gave me a bath, and I waited on her bed for her to fix my hair. She carried in a stack of pillowcases and stuffed pillows, fluffy as clouds, inside them. My father carried in a box, put it down, turned from side to side showing off his muscles like a weightlifting champion, and said, "Who's the man?"

"You are, darling," my mother said, as if he'd been home helping her unpack all day.

My father lay down next to me bare-chested and pulled the sheets to his waist.

"I want to comb your hair," I said, pointing to his chest." Raking the comb through his black curls, I said, "See, no knots."

With sweet eyes my father looked at my mother, and then he smiled at me. "You're right, my love. No knots at all."

I ran to my room and got my free chicken hat and the plastic egg with the chick inside. I climbed back into bed between my parents and because of all I'd been through they let me stay. Smiling in the dark, I wore my chicken hat and cradled the egg.

ᒐ THE JOKER

H e pinned her arms above her head. Callie squirmed beneath him. He brought his face close to hers and stuck his tongue out as if to lick her, then pulled back.

He tickled her. Callie thrashed on Mama's bed, messing the coverlet, and I was petrified she'd ruin it. I got in trouble last week for eating chips in Mama's bed. I left crumbs behind, and they jabbed at her all night long. She didn't like people horsing around on her bed. And it wouldn't matter if it was Daddy's fault that their blanket got messed up. She'd still go crazy when she saw.

He reached for a jump rope off his architect table and giggled like the Joker as he tied Callie's hands behind her back. Callie yanked at the fastened rope. I sat behind them cross-legged on the blue velvet chair, and watched. "Stay there, Willow," he said to me. And I didn't move.

He uncovered a gold cylinder and red lipstick shot up, a flash of vibrancy. He drew close to Callie and marked her cheeks. First the right and then the left. Red lines like scars ran along her face, and we giggled at the absurdity. He loved to play like a boy. "Silly, Daddy."

The humidity was fierce, like it always was that time of year in New Orleans, and the mirror behind his bed became foggy, our images blurred. He raised his finger and swept it down the center. "Come here, Willow." And I climbed on his bed. "Careful," he said.

"You're on this side," he said to me. "And Callie, you're on this side." He untied her, and the jump rope lay like a snake dividing the coverlet. "There are alligators down there," he said, eyeing the carpet. "Don't fall in." He looked at both of us, one and then the other. "When I say three you can start playing but don't cross the line," he said, pointing to it. "Or you lose."

⌒ BLIND MAN'S BLUFF

Hungry, I look in our kitchen closet for something to eat. It's difficult to see since the light went out a few days ago, but I can still make out a box of bread crumbs, a bag of sugar, French's Yellow Mustard, and a can of coffee.

My brother has learned from me to hide the good stuff in the back on top, so I step onto the bottom shelf and lift myself up. The fingers on my left hand cling to the top shelf holding me, while my right hand skims over sticky contact paper searching for anything acceptable—a cookie, a bag of chips, some raisins.

Reaching far back into the darkness, I find something that feels familiar. In my excitement, I jump down from the shelf with the bag held tight, and my elbow hits the frame of the door. It hurts. My arm feels numb, and it takes me a few seconds before I realize that the bag I've found is empty, and I know my brother got the last Oreo. My instinct is to complain, but there's nobody home for me to complain to. I storm out the back door, hearing the screen slam behind me.

The bright sun burns my eyes, and I look down, staring at my pink Keds as I walk, one foot in front of the other, toward Willow's house.

Willow is my best friend and our backyards connect. Our ranch-style houses share a well-traveled path lined with blooming trees, now wet with the smell of soil. The greenery brushes against me as I shuffle from my house to hers. Separating the yards, at the end of the path, there is a broken fence with a hole in it, splintered from years of exposure to sun and rain.

When I crawl through the fence, Willow is there. She looks up from what she is doing and says, "Hi."

"Hi," I say, moving toward her.

"Look," she says as she points to a doodlebug. "When you touch it, it curls."

I touch the doodlebug and watch it curl into its shell.

"Do you want to go inside?" Willow asks as she stands, and I wonder if she can read my mind.

Willow's mother makes us drink milk with lunch, peanut butter and jelly on white bread. I watch as she cuts the ends off the bread, an act that seems natural and foreign at once. The house smells of garlic and home cooking, and I can almost taste what she stirs in the pots beside her.

Later Willow suggests that we polish our fingernails. We ask her older sister, Ashley, if we can use her polish. Ashley is a cheerleader, and she wears her short green-and-white uniform like a trophy. She has big boobs and a boyfriend and in between football games and varsity parties, she tells me things she thinks I should know—like how to take care of my frizzy brown hair by putting my head in between my knees, brushing all of my hair to the top of my head, attaching a ponytail holder there, and rolling the dangling hair onto an extra-large roller or an empty vegetable can, with both ends cut off for the bobby pins. Given the recent humidity, this is invaluable information, and when I part my hair down the middle after taking care of it in this way, I no longer look like Bozo the Clown.

"A girl should always look her best," Ashley says. And she always does, never relaxing long enough to let her hair curl or her mascara wear off.

Willow's sister doesn't tell me these things out of kindness. I think she likes how I look at her, how I study her every move. She gives me these beauty tips as though they are facts, definite, like a theorem, if a = b, and b = c, then a = c. But I'm not convinced, even if I bother to follow all her beauty advice, that I will be beautiful too.

She lets us use her polish and I paint one finger bright orange; the next, fire engine red; and the next, wine, and then start over again, bright orange, fire engine red, wine. I am content with this attempt at creativity until Willow looks at what I am doing and snickers.

"Oh, you did a pattern." She tilts her head so that the hair around the front of her face covers her eyes, and she smirks. "You are so predictable."

She drags out the word "so" just long enough to make me feel stupid.

"I don't like to be *so* obvious, she continues."

Again, she says the word "so" like it has four syllables, and looks down at her nails, which are polished haphazardly, a different design on each nail.

Ashley has great albums, which we're not allowed to touch, but when she goes out, Willow and I sneak into her room to get them. We play the music loudly, confident that she won't be home for hours.

In our hands, we hold fake microphones and mouth every word.

My body moves to the music freely, at least as freely as can be expected for a kid in private school whose parents vote Republican and drive a Cadillac.

With closed eyes I dream of my teacher, Mr. Kelvidge, who every Friday devotes the last half hour of class to music. He sits on the rug with us, bent over his guitar, strumming, and we sing "Blowin' in the Wind," reading from sheets he's handed out. As I dance, my mind wanders and I recall him leaning over me, pointing to a faraway place on the world map, and I smell his long wavy hair, a commitment to freedom, love, and peace.

In the late afternoon, we watch *The Brady Bunch*, our favorite show, and return to the kitchen for a snack. There are warm cookies on a tray and Willow's mother, tall and blonde, serves them to us at the table. She walks to the other end of the kitchen, and I pay attention to the sound her slip-on heels make as they hit the tile floor. She is wearing skintight black leggings and a short top that ties in the back. Positioned behind the sink on the windowsill there is a radio, and she turns it on. Soft music plays in the background, and she reaches for her pack of cigarettes and her lighter. She lights up, throwing her head back before she exhales. She places the cigarette on the edge of the white Formica counter, and I watch as it burns. She dices onions on a cutting board, stopping every few seconds to lift her cigarette to her mouth, allowing the ash to grow, becoming impossibly long, and hanging, threatening collapse. I'm certain the ash will fall when she runs the water and puts the cigarette out in the sink. She moves back to the cutting board and continues to chop. Tears collect in the corners of her eyes, and she uses the back of her hand to wipe them as they cascade down her cheek. She leans and stirs what simmers on the stove.

"Does that hurt?" I ask.

She picks her head up and looks at me.

"Does what hurt?"

"You're crying."

She laughs, "I'm not crying."

Running a finger along the knife, she detaches stuck onions and moves the cutting board away, to the other end of the counter.

"The onions burn my eyes, that's all."

Just then, Mr. Johnson, Willow's father, appears in the kitchen. He shuts off the radio and stands next to his wife. "What's for dinner?"

"Soup," Willow's mother answers.

"I can see it's soup. What kind of soup?"

Willow's mother stops stirring and she rests the spoon on the counter. She covers the pot with its lid and relocates herself away from the stove.

"Pea soup," she answers gently as she glances at us and smiles.

SUNLIGHT disappears from the sky as if a giant eraser has come and erased the light away. Darkness approaches against my wishes. Although I know I must go home, I hesitate.

Outside the sky is purple. The wind feels fresh on my skin, and I talk to God as I cross the backyard. It's not like I talk about anything important; it's not religious in any way, it's not even a prayer, it's just that I know He's there. If anyone saw me doing this, they'd think I was crazy, so I speak without moving my lips. Like a ventriloquist's, the voice comes from within, but I am sure that He hears me.

The back door is not locked, and I walk inside. There are no lights on. I feel for the switch and brighten the room. The screen door slams behind me, and everything inside feels still.

I call through the house, "Mom?"

She's not in the kitchen or the den.

"Dad?" I'm hopeful as I continue past the bedrooms, but no one answers.

My younger brother doesn't hear me calling. He's in his room with the door closed. I peek in to find he's sitting in the dark watching *Star Trek*. Without turning his head, he says, "Mom and Dad went out to eat. They'll be back at nine. JoAnne's babysitting."

By now it's dark outside, and I'm hungry again. I open the freezer door the way Bob Barker opens Door Number Two for his contestants. As a contestant chooses a trip to Hawaii, a set of dishes, a car, or a washer/dryer combination, I choose from tall, neat stacks of Swanson's dinners: Hungry-Man turkey, macaroni and cheese, Swedish meatballs, or chicken pot pie.

THE next day is hot and sticky, nearly one hundred degrees Fahrenheit. I stroll through our backyard, stopping to touch blossoms on our trees. I pull a bud from its stem and petals unfold, revealing its center. Crawling through the hole in our fence, I emerge on the other side, in Willow's backyard, and notice for the first time that it's getting more difficult for me to fit.

Willow and I drift to her front lawn and sit under a tree, Indian style. We watch a family move into the house down the block and searching for clues, we scrutinize their belongings—sofas, paintings, and night tables—as they are unloaded from a truck and carried into their new home.

Willow takes a piece of gum from her pocket and begins to unwrap it.

"Can I have a piece?"

"It's my last one," Willow says.

I remind her that just yesterday I shared my last piece. She lifts her eyebrows in disbelief.

"You gave me the smallest crumb, it was nothing."

Snickering, she sticks out her tongue, frog-like, and holds the gum near the tip of it. She waits just long enough to make me think she might change her mind before she devours it. The gum folds as it enters her mouth.

I look away, absorbing my anger the way a paper towel absorbs spilled juice. I don't say a word. The silence lies between us, heavy and unyielding. Out of the corner of my eye I can see Willow looking at me, waiting for the chance to bring me back in.

"Let's go there," she says, as she points down the block to our new neighbors.

I'm willing to let the uncomfortable moment pass for two reasons. One, I like the idea of spying on our new neighbors, and two, I don't want to push Willow too far. If I stay angry, Willow will accuse me of making a big deal out of nothing, and she'll snap. I can envision her face, eyes narrowing, the top and bottom lids almost touching, nostrils flaring, and I can hear what she'll say.

"So why do you stay with me if I'm so mean? Why don't you just go home?"

We walk down the block toward our new neighbors and see a boy near the side of the house. Head down, he's leaning against the red brick.

"He's cute," Willow whispers, covering her mouth with her hand.

He has golden skin and while the sun seems to have darkened his body it has lightened his hair, leaving streaks of sunshine that dangle freely in front of his face. I can feel my heart pumping through my chest, and I'm actually afraid that this is noticeable.

He looks at us as we pass by. Willow squeezes my hand and giggles.

"Did you see that? He looked right at me."

Instantly there is a game that I'm not part of.

He approaches us, and I wonder what it would be like to touch his hair, his arms. He tells us his name is Andrew, and Willow shares elaborate stories about herself and the neighborhood while I stumble over my words, not sure of what I want to say.

Later, I watch as Willow gets ready to go back to Andrew's house that night. She puts on a tank top, tight blue jeans, and Dr. Scholl's sandals. I think she looks great, but she doesn't stop there, applying light-blue eye shadow, rouge, and lip gloss to her face as though she's a painter adding the final touches to her masterpiece.

She takes her time accentuating her eyes with thick black eyeliner and layers and layers of black Maybelline mascara, making sure to separate and lengthen each lash. She plugs in her blow dryer and tugs on her already straight and shiny hair.

I stare at her image in the mirror.

I'm not allowed to wear makeup, but I put on lip gloss anyway.

When it's dark, Willow and I go back to Andrew's house. Our parents don't mind. They think it's nice that we have made friends with the new neighbors.

There is a light hanging off the side of the garage,

casting a stream of yellow down a narrow path, and we follow it to Andrew's backyard.

He's lying down on a huge trampoline, and he lifts his head to greet us. We climb up and join him. There is a pack of cigarettes, an ashtray, and a lighter resting next to him. I look the other way, rigid, pretending that this is no reason to be alarmed. Willow, on the other hand, reaches for the pack and, before I know it, she is lying back, propped on an elbow, blowing large masses of smoke into the air, letting down her inhibitions the way Rapunzel lets down her hair. Andrew lies next to her and shows off by blowing rings inside of rings.

The smoke circles above me, cloud-like.

Andrew puts out his cigarette and reaches for Willow. They kiss. I try not to watch their heads moving back and forth but I'm hypnotized by the motion. I put myself inside of Willow, inside her skin, feeling his lips on mine.

Wishing their braces would get stuck together, I announce I'm going home.

In bed I lie awake, thinking about Willow and what she's done. Thoughts mix in my mind growing muddier like finger paint across wet paper. I question our friendship.

In the morning Willow calls bright and early.

"Wakey, wakey," she chirps into the phone. "Are you up yet?"

"What time is it?" I answer flatly.

"It's almost eight. I have to talk to you."

I open my eyes just enough to see the numbers on my clock. It is 7:22.

"Haven't I asked you not to wake me up?"

"Yes, but this is important. Andrew and I kissed."

"I know. I was there."

"What did you expect me to do? I didn't know he was going to kiss me."

"You could have warned me," I said, wrapping myself inside my blanket.

"You really need to grow up, Callie. It's not a big deal."

At this point I know that if I keep this going Willow will be angrier at me than I am at her.

"Now, do you want to hear about what happened last night or should I call Sally and Katy?"

I don't answer.

"Anyway," she tries one last time, "I want to show you something. It's a secret. Come over."

I decide to go there, knowing that I wouldn't miss this, and as I put the receiver down, I wonder why she always has to wake me up so early.

Our friends Sally and Katy are in the kitchen eating peanut butter and jelly sandwiches when I get there. Willow has already told them about the night before, punishing me for being late. She pretends like she has no intention of sharing the events of her night with me, and I pretend I don't care, when we both know she'll tell me everything, with details she didn't tell Sally and Katy.

Willow's mother offers me a sandwich, and the four of us sit around the kitchen table like little old ladies playing canasta, inebriated with friendship.

When Willow is ready, Sally, Katy, and I follow her to her room, which has recently been decorated with plush, wall-to-wall pink carpet. In the center of the room, there is a queen-size bed and night tables the color of canned asparagus.

"Do you want to know my secret?" Willow asks as we lie across her bed, talking. "I'm not supposed to show anyone, but I don't care." And she makes each one of us swear not to tell.

Willow pushes a night table away from the wall, revealing a door that is covered in the same patterned wallpaper that decorates the rest of her room. The pattern continues over the door uninterrupted, leaving no sign that the wall has been cut there.

"Behind the door there is a tunnel," Willow whispers. "It leads to my parents' room."

Willow squats and runs her open hand along the edges of the door.

"My father did this for me. If a burglar tries to come into our house I just crawl through the tunnel to his room, to the inside of his closet."

Sally and Katy think the tunnel is fascinating, and I, in a moment of jealousy and longing, wish that my father had thought about such protection for me.

Sally's a goody-goody, but Katy's always breaking the rules, and she dares Willow to go through it. Willow reminds us that her father will go crazy if he finds out she's told us about the tunnel.

We don't want to aggravate Willow's father. There's something unusual about him, tall and stiff like the buildings he creates; he reads *Playboy* while he chain-smokes at the architect's table in his bedroom. A lamp curls up from the desktop and down over his work. The lamp is on all hours of the night while he paces back and forth, up and down the hallways. His bedroom door is never closed. He is always awake.

We hang out in Willow's room for a while. Sunlight pours through the window, leaving a streak across her bed. The sky is a brilliant blue.

"Let's go for a walk," I suggest, needing to feel the warmth.

The four of us have traveled halfway around the block when the driver of a small brown car, beat-up and dirty, pulls up next to us.

He stretches his thick neck in our direction as he wipes the sweat from his unshaven face with the back of his hand, and calls to us.

"Do you girls know where Crystal Street is?"

Katy and Sally stay back, and I'm tentative too about approaching the car with its driver's fleshy arm overflowing from his vehicle like rising dough in a bowl, but Willow steps forward. I follow. The car vibrates to the beat of the blasting music, and although an air freshener disguised as a Christmas tree dangles from his rearview mirror, the smell of stale cigarettes permeates the air. Willow begins to explain how to get to Crystal Street when I notice that one of his hands is on the steering wheel and the other is on his exposed flesh, stroking himself as he speaks to us.

I'm scared, but I stay calm, too afraid to act. Willow stays cool, too, and I wonder if she sees. I keep my eyes glued to his, unable to look down while Willow gestures toward Crystal Street. The man thanks us and drives away slowly.

The four of us run through a backyard and on to the next street. We hide behind a thick wall of bushes, bending low to stay out of sight.

"Listen," Willow says. "He's going to come back. I know it. He's going to come back."

Willow struggles to remain calm but it's clear she's scared, terrified even. I have never seen Willow afraid before.

From behind the bushes we watch as the man drives past us. We wait together in the shaded foliage for some time before we run back to Willow's house, back to safety.

We don't tell anyone what's happened. Willow makes us promise.

THE next morning, I wake up to find my mother reading the newspaper and drinking coffee at the dinette table. My father is playing golf and my brother is watching cartoons.

Amongst the frozen dinners there are breakfast choices as well: frozen waffles, sausages, and biscuits. I decide on Poppin' Fresh Biscuits and put them in the oven to bake.

"What are you going to do today?" my mother asks, not lifting her eyes from behind the newspaper.

"I don't know."

"Oh," she says, and continues to read.

I eat breakfast and watch cartoons. At noon I get dressed, and the back door slams behind me as I head for the yard. I get down on all fours and inhale to make myself smaller, still trying to fit through the opening in the fence. Standing up on the other side, I remove the twigs and grass from my stained, bare knees, and trace the impressions left on my skin with a finger.

Sally and Katy are with Willow in her room when I get there. Willow wants to play inside given the humidity. She hates to sweat when it isn't absolutely necessary.

They want to play blind man's bluff, and so Willow closes the blinds to make it dark in her room. Small specks of light manage to penetrate through the aluminum slats and I find myself hiding in front of the secret tunnel. I keep staring at it, feeling for the place where the wallpaper ends and then begins again. The darkness scares me and I hold my breath as Willow walks by, blindfolded. I try to escape by rolling on the bed.

She stands up tall and rips the blindfold from her face. "I got you!"

"You did not!" I yell back.

I turn on the light and see the red in Willow's face. Her anger takes over, and her distorted expression frightens me more than the darkness did.

"I did too. I felt you go by," she insists.

"You didn't touch me," I say, standing up to meet her glaring eyes.

"Yes I did, you liar."

"You did not, Willow." But I say this with less conviction, and Willow can sense weakness.

Sally and Katy agree with Willow, and I feel defeated by their judgment.

"I quit!" I yell.

As I close the door behind me it occurs to me that I have nowhere to go. I'm sure no one is at my house. I wish my friends would beg me to stay.

Alone in the hallway I hear another angry voice. I walk closer to the noise, clinging to the wall. Through their open bedroom door, I see Willow's father holding her mother's arm and twisting it so that she is forced to go down on her knees. Tears spill from her eyes, and she begs her husband to let go.

"You're hurting me," she cries.

"How many times have I told you not to answer me that way? I warned you, but you never listen."

He is towering over her, spit flying from his mouth as he reprimands her, twisting her like clay. He drags her by the hair across the room to his worktable, to the lamp that is always on.

I back away and then lean in further so I can see.

He smashes her face into the magazine that lies open on the table.

"You never learn," he says.

He pinches her cheeks between his hands and shakes her hard.

"Do you?"

He rolls the magazine into a tube and swats at her as if she were a fly. She crawls around their bedroom floor trying to break away, one arm raised as a shield, soiling the white wall-to-wall carpet with her misery.

I shut my eyes and shake my head hard as if I can shake the image of Willow's whimpering mother out of my mind.

When I turn around, Willow is there. Black tears well and fall from her eyes. I look down, unsure of what to do. Neither one of us moves, and then I reach for her the way a mother does for her child. Hugging, we inhale and exhale together, sharing in that moment what connects us. After a few minutes I need to step away, but Willow follows, staying close. Her hair is caught on my earring, and we are stuck together, face to face. I lift my hand to wipe her tears as she works to unravel her hair. When we finally part I take Willow by the hand and lead her to the kitchen. She washes her face.

"Now you know," she says.

"It's OK."

"Swear you won't tell anyone."

"I swear."

"Does it look like I've been crying?"

"No. You look fine."

We walk back down the hallway to her room. I don't hesitate. I know I will continue to go to Willow's house. I will continue to eat peanut butter and jelly sandwiches around her kitchen table, steal and burn report cards as they arrive in the mail, and invent creative ways to hide the marks the boys in the neighborhood leave on her neck.

There is music coming from Willow's room, and I envision Katy and Sally singing and dancing wildly, holding fake microphones and wearing high heels. I lift my hand to touch my aching ear. I didn't feel the pain before, but now my ear is throbbing.

We stop right outside of Willow's bedroom door, and Willow looks deep into my eyes as if to remind me this is our little secret. She opens the door to her room, and I am taken by the festivity, the room bursting with music and dance.

Katy moves towards us and screams over the music, "Where were you?"

Willow doesn't answer. She boogies into the room as if a question has not been asked.

Within moments, as if nothing has changed, we are all singing and dancing to Elton John's "Goodbye Yellow Brick Road," and as I dance, I hold my earlobe between two fingers, rubbing gently, and think about the day Willow and I got our ears pierced. She insisted on going first and sat motionless as the woman at the jewelry counter marked her ear with a black pen. The woman held the gun that would fire a fourteen-karat gold earring into her ear, and I held her hand until it was done.

ꝯ ALL YOU TOUCH

I sat with my seat reclined as far back as possible, could barely see out the windshield. My left foot was up on the seat next to me. The windows were down; the air, sweet. The smell stirred up the soul—the passion of New Orleans. Music blasted, and Willow and I sang that song by Supertramp, "The Logical Song." Carefree, we cruised over the expressway past Lakewood South.

"That must be it," Willow said.

"Where?" I asked.

"Over there, upstairs." She pointed to a two-story building that appeared abandoned.

"Are you crazy? Who are these guys?"

"I told you. I met them last night."

"You met them at a bar, Willow. This is crazy."

I pulled around to the side of the building and parked. The dilapidated structure was behind a gas station, and while this was concerning, I was more intrigued by who lived inside. It was cool we were meeting new people, especially boys, so I took out my purse and stared into the rearview mirror, outlined my lips with dark liner, then applied a coat of shimmering gold gloss.

"Let me use that," Willow said.

I handed her the gloss, dug in my purse for my brush, and fixed my hair.

"Are you ready?" she asked.

"Do I look ready?" I threw my head forward. My hair danced around my face, and I puckered up.

"Come on," she said, and she opened the car door.

Everything was foreign to me. A stray dog wandered the yard. Weeds grew out of control up the path. There was no grass, only dirt and rocks. We walked to a narrow staircase, and Willow led the way up. I looked around as if on watch. The stairs were rickety, and I paid attention to each step. Willow knocked on the frame of the screen door. From a back room Pink Floyd played.

A boy with shoulder-length blond hair, who must've been about eighteen, came to the door. He wore blue jeans real low and baggy. A white tank top covered his long, skinny body but left his arms exposed. They were muscular and tan—smooth, too. I wasn't used to that. My dad and all my uncles were covered like bears with fur, hair on their backs, inside their ears, and on their knuckles.

"Callie, this is Wayne."

"Hi," I said.

"Hello." And I noticed how he dragged this out. In a hospitable southern kind of way, he said, "Welcome to our humble abode." He stepped aside, inviting us in. Straight ahead hung a *Dark Side of the Moon* poster.

Willow strutted across the room, swinging her arms and swaying her hips as though she'd been there before. I walked behind her and stumbled on a bump in the carpet. I straightened myself quickly, and nobody seemed to notice.

The couch was low to the ground and lopsided. Willow and I sat on it. Wayne sat on a folding chair across from us. The coffee table was cluttered: an ashtray from Pat O'Brien's, dirty shot glasses, empty beer bottles, and a pack of Marlboros.

"Hey, John," Wayne screamed over the music. "Where are you? The girls are here."

"I'll be right there."

"Y'all been living here long?" Willow asked in a long, slow drawl.

"No," Wayne said, pushing hair from his face. "We just moved in two months ago. My stepdad's an asshole." He leaned forward, lifted the pack of cigarettes, and took one out. "He tried to run my life like he runs my mother's. Don't need that shit." He sat back in his chair, and I watched as he allowed the cigarette to hang from the corner of his mouth, from the tip of his lips. I thought I'd never seen lips so nice before. He was cute, I had to admit. He lit up with a lighter he pulled from his back pocket. He took a deep breath, closed his eyes, and the smoke curled around his face. "So I left," he said.

I looked down and tried to appear as if I understood this, as if leaving home were a normal thing to do. I was sitting there feeling kind of strange—you know, a little scared, I guess. And I wondered what his friend would be like. I mean, Willow met them first, so it was pretty much for sure that her guy would be cuter than mine. But just so long as mine was cute, it didn't matter. That's just the way it was with me and Willow; she always got the cuter guy.

The first thing John said when he finally came into the room was that he was sorry to keep two beautiful girls like us waiting. He meant it, too. He wasn't trying to be all suave and stupid like those guys on TV. He was really sorry. He said he couldn't find a clean shirt. I wondered about that, you know, living on your own, responsible for your own laundry, never having clean clothes. At my house the clothes were always put back in my drawers. JoAnne, our housekeeper, really knew what she was doing. The whites —real white, neatly folded or hung up. I could leave my clothes sprawled out across my bedroom floor, which I did, and it wouldn't matter. I realized then that you never know how lucky you are until something like this reaches up from nowhere and grabs you, wraps its arms around you, and makes you think. Something as stupid as having your clothes picked up off the floor, cleaned, and put back in the drawer. Something as ordinary as having a mother and father, I mean, your own mother and father actually living in the same house together.

He stood right in front of me, put out his hand like a real gentleman, and said, "My name is John. Nice to meet you."

I looked up at him and reached my hand toward his. "I'm Callie." His hand felt big and strong, and I was glad to shake it. He was cute. Not as cute as Wayne—I mean he had brown hair, not blond—but it was long and wavy like Wayne's, and his body was cool, all big and hairless and everything. But most importantly, I liked his eyes. He had real nice eyes, dark and large but mostly kind, the sort of eyes that make you feel safe even when you probably shouldn't. You could know certain things, count on certain things from someone's eyes. He had an earring in his ear and a tattoo on his arm—a lightning bolt. I thought it was cool. I'd never met a boy with an earring and a tattoo before.

He asked if we wanted anything to drink. Willow said she'd have a beer, so I said I'd have one, too. I didn't really drink—didn't really like the taste but I wanted to try. It was time. Everyone I knew had been drinking for a while already, and frankly I was feeling kind of nervous. I mean this was nothing too familiar for me and I needed some-thing, like they say on TV and like I'd heard my parents say a million times, "to take the edge off."

I watched John, watched him move, as he got the beer out of the refrigerator. He brought a six-pack back to the table, opened a can, and handed it to me. Then he opened another and handed it to Willow. He gave one to Wayne before claiming his own, and I was sure he was a real nice person. I took a sip of beer. I felt like getting drunk.

Willow asked where the bathroom was, and she left me alone with them.

"So where do y'all go to school?" I asked.

"School, what's that?" Wayne laughed and leaned so far back in his chair, I thought he might fall.

"I dropped out," John said.

"Really," I said, shaking my head as if I agreed. I took another sip of beer and wondered if I was pulling this off.

"I left after eighth grade. Needed money, you know. Needed to get on with my life."

I didn't know what to say. I wasn't much of a conver-sationalist.

Wayne jumped up out of his seat. "Come on, let's get out of here."

Willow appeared next to him. "Where do you want to go?"

"Let's go for a ride."

The four of us got into my car and headed for the lake-front. Through the rearview mirror, I could see Wayne and Willow kissing. I tried to focus on the road but every once in a while, my eyes were drawn to them. I changed the ra-dio station. John was a good talker, and I was thankful for that. He told me about how he met Wayne at the Red Lobster on Veteran's Avenue. Wayne was a waiter there, and he always gave John extra shrimp, free. They became friends, and when they moved into the apartment near the gas station, John got a job there. He told me that he wanted to do something else with his life, but he wasn't sure what yet.

By the time we got to the lakefront, it was completely dark outside. I'd never been there at night before. The grass was wet and so were my toes inside my Candie's. I hated when that happened, but I kept walking as if I didn't mind that or the fact that each time I stepped, the heel, like a drill, dug up the earth. There were lights in the distance from the grand water fountain—colored lights of purple, blue, and gold. But that was in the distance.

It took time for our eyes to adjust. Wayne pulled out his lighter and held it in front of us. We followed single file, holding hands.

I liked holding John's hand. It felt right. I mean, it was weird that he was nineteen and I was only fifteen, but I didn't feel younger—not too much younger, anyway. He turned to warn me about a ditch in the ground. He was taking care of me, and I wanted him to.

We set out a sheet, each taking a corner. White, it arched like a sail before hitting the ground. Wayne laid out cigarettes, a lighter, and a bottle of wine. We drank out of the bottle, passing it around. Boone's Farm strawberry.

Wayne put his arm around Willow, and before I knew it they were making out again. They lay down together, stretched out across the sheet. In the darkness it was hard to see, and I tried not to look, but Wayne's white T-shirt moved like a glow-in-the-dark toy.

John and I sat side by side, Indian style, not facing them. We took turns sipping the wine, and then John stood, the wine bottle in one hand, my hand in his other. We walked away from Willow and Wayne, saying nothing.

It was quiet. We were alone. And it occurred to me again that I didn't really know John. He seemed nice and all, had those trusting eyes, but really he was a stranger. He could hurt me, and it would be my own fault. And I could hear my parents saying, "Didn't we tell you not to talk to strangers?" My brother would say, "You're an idiot." And the worst part was, I knew they'd be right. I mean, what was I doing there? No one but Willow knew where I was, and she was way too distracted to notice me or my absence. For all I knew, John could be a madman, an ax murderer, or a serial killer. But for some reason, with no apparent legitimacy, I trusted him, trusted myself to know he was kind. He put his arm around me, and I could see out of the corner of my eye that he was looking at me. I knew that if I turned my head toward his, he'd kiss me. Completely aware of something pulling inside me, a force I had not experienced before, I faced him. He pressed his lips on mine, and I felt their warmth.

Gently, he guided me down so that we lay on the wet grass. He breathed in deeply and kissed me again, lips parted, and our tongues touched. For a moment I got lost in the swirling, lost in the movement, but it wasn't long before I came to and wondered if he thought I was a good kisser. I wasn't even sure he was a good kisser, but it felt nice, so I relaxed again and assumed we were doing it right.

John moved his hand, and I was afraid he'd try to do something else. I mean, I was OK up until that point but I wasn't ready for more. He seemed to know that because he didn't even try.

He turned onto his back. "Aren't the stars amazing?

Art in the sky." He raised his arm, pointing his finger to the sky as if it were a brush and he were the artist. "See the three stars together, the ones in a row?"

I wasn't sure I knew what he was looking at, but I said yes anyway.

"Those three stars are the belt of Orion. He's the sun god. The destroyer of darkness."

"How do you know that?"

"My mother's a fortune-teller. She knows things about the stars, the sun, and the moon." He waved his arms as if he could hold the sky, encompass it all. "When I was small she told me stories of gods and goddesses. The stories took me away from the fighting. My stepdad was always fighting with someone about something."

"Where's your mom now?"

"She lives in Shreveport. My stepdad's the kind of guy that sits around drinking beer in a white T-shirt all day. No job, no interests. A real piece of work, the asshole sits around all day watching television and spends the money my Mama earns."

He moved closer to me and whispered in my ear. "Artemis was the goddess of wild animals, and she fell for Orion."

John raised himself up on his elbow to look at me, and it felt like something inside me was acknowledged and opened. I envisioned myself touching him, tracing the lightning bolt, a zigzag up his arm.

"The problem was," John continued, "that Artemis had a brother named Apollo, and he didn't like that his sister had fallen in love."

I listened as John told me how Apollo wanted to destroy Orion and how he did.

"When Orion died, Artemis was real sad. She put his dead body in her chariot and brought him to the sky. She found the darkest place so that his stars would shine the brightest."

"That is so sad," I said.

"Love never goes right, anyway."

"How can you say that?"

"That's how I see it."

"Not me."

"You're sweet." He kissed me smack on the lips. "You're special, too. A goddess, right here on earth," he said, and wrapped me in his large arms. We lay there quietly for some time before he looked back up at the sky. "You believe the sun god lives up there?"

I wasn't sure what to say. I mean, I believed in God, but not necessarily a sun god. I thought there was one God who could do it all. But I decided then that I loved people like John. People who believed in magic, people who told stories. So I said, "Sure, why not?"

I recognized in John a tortured soul, lost but journeying toward light. I mean, he wasn't miserable or anything, but he wanted the world to be a certain way, and it wasn't. So when I say tortured, I really mean disappointed. Disappointed in the ugly ways of the world.

He pulled me close to him and I closed my eyes, preparing for what would follow. I felt fear and desire, the mix a pleasure so deep and delicious it was difficult to catch my own breath. When his lips touched mine, I was brought to a new place, a place far away and my very own. I felt free and yet connected. Captivated by what I believed was his goodness, his spirit, I wanted to be a part of his world.

After a few minutes we stopped kissing and even though my face hurt, raw from kissing for so long, I reached for him, wanting more, wanting this journey to last forever. Opening my eyes, I put my hands through his hair and found his mouth.

Across the night sky, stars—vast as possibility.

ℒ HAPPILY EVER AFTER

Once upon a time, there was a girl who was enchanted by a boy who drove a Porsche. The boy handled his car up hills and around sharp curves like a young man who knew what he wanted.

"I love this car," he shouted over the engine, as he pressed the gas pedal all the way down.

The boy washed his car every day with a soapy towel, reached his arms across the hood, caressing the doors, massaging the windows.

When he started the engine, the boy sang out in joy while he grabbed the stick shift and released the clutch and pulled out onto the open road. Clear blue sky above, he drove, flooring it, designer sunglasses covering his face.

His white Porsche was fast—faster than tradition or feeling, faster than sorrow or pain. And the boy loved his car, and the roar of the engine, and how swiftly he could move, almost fly.

The girl was wild about this boy who drove a Porsche. One sunny day she asked him, "Why this car?"

"Are you kidding?" he sneered, and his eyebrows met in the center of his forehead like two caterpillars convening.

The girl saw the boy was annoyed. "But there are other nice cars," she persisted, draping her body along the exterior of his Porsche.

"Not for me," he answered, looking away.

The boy thundered across the city. He soared on the FDR, going nearly ninety miles per hour, and held the stick shift tightly, laughing like a child playing a driving game at the arcade. Wind whisked by, enveloping him as he cruised toward the horizon; the music, like his spirit, bursting. He had all he wanted.

But he did think the girl was pretty in her black leather pants, her body shiny and sleek like his Porsche. And he adored that she listened when he spoke of his car. He was unaware that while they drank champagne at a fancy French restaurant, she gazed past him and saw herself in the mirror. She looked her best, and she thought he looked sharp, too. Peering into his eyes, inspecting him, she saw their future and all that she aimed to possess. But when the night was over, he drove her home and took off, speeding, leaving her there alone.

The next night, the girl couldn't find him, and she listened for the roar of his engine, far off, and she followed the sound to a lavish party, a black-tie affair, where they danced all night. They danced until her feet hurt, and she cursed her brand-new designer shoes. After midnight he drove her home and left her there alone, again driving off, soaring toward freedom, tasting wind.

Like a weed, obsession grew inside her, and she couldn't tolerate the pace any longer, never knowing when he'd drive off, never knowing when she'd see his light-filled eyes and his crooked grin that showed his dimples, long and deep, like her desire.

She went to the beauty parlor. She had a manicure, a pedicure, and a facial. She had her eyebrows waxed, and her hair blown straight. She bought a low-cut blouse and a push-up bra. She added rouge and shadow, lip gloss and mascara.

"Hi," she said.

"Hi," he replied. But he did not lift his head as he waxed his car.

He was driving her crazy. She dreamed of his hands on either side of her waist, steering her.

Driven, she devised a plan to destroy the car, determined to ruin it and replace one passion with another. When it was dark, she used a key and scratched into his Porsche. Digging deep, she left marks, as if she had clawed into the boy himself, and he gasped at the sight of his damaged car. She held him, wrapping him in her arms. But he broke away, hurt.

He set about to repairing the gashes, more like wounds. And his devotion to his car and all that he loved kept him further from the girl.

"Get rid of the car," she told her friend. "I'll leave the key outside."

She called the boy and asked him to come over. She listened to stories about his car, and that distracted him while she lifted his key from the coffee table. Maneuvering him away from the window, her plan was put into motion.

This time when the boy tried to leave her, he found his car was gone. Freedom, with all its speed and potential, had driven off, leaving him there lost. Outside of her house, the boy howled. Gigantic tears and a puddle of sorrow collected around him. Devastated, he looked up to the heavens and saw the girl, a halo of yellow light around her, brushing her hair near the open window. She unfolded her curls, and they cascaded down the side of her house toward him. He held fast to her locks and she brought him to her as if she were a fairy-tale heroine. She held him in her arms, clinging to him.

When the sun came up, he followed the tire marks

around the city, into the country, through the forest, up hills, until far away he finally heard the engine calling his name. He got into his car and drove all day and into the night, bewitched.

The next day he woke to clean his car, stroking it; his arms circled three times to the left and three times to the right, washing away unhappiness. The white Porsche shone more than ever.

Propelled by passion, the girl was determined to capture his heart, and she plotted to possess it. She gathered her strength, summoned her powers, and, waiting for the right time, used a sledgehammer as if it were a magic wand. She threw her arms back behind her head and then, like a pendulum, she swung them forward, crashing her weapon, with its heavy metal head, against his car's side-view mirror. The mirror fell to the floor, shattering, and broken pieces lay on the ground, reflecting the sun. She strolled around to the other side of his car. Without hesitation, she lifted the sledgehammer with both hands and launched a blow with the vigor of lust at the other side-view mirror, cracking it. With a knife she slashed the tires and collected the strips of black rubber as if she were collecting shapes for a collage. She snapped off the windshield wipers like the breaking of chopsticks, knocked off the steering wheel, and then detached the rearview mirror.

Convinced she had the right-of-way, routed toward her desire, she started the engine and watched the fumes rise. She stared at the needle as it moved from full to empty, the yellow light on. It crossed her mind to activate the blinker signal but decided against it because she had no intention of turning around. She'd gone too far.

Her friend, draped in black, now had a mustache over

his thin pink lips and he showed up again, as promised. He lifted the hood of the white Porsche, and with his tools, he removed the heart of her problem. The engine lay silent on the ground.

She had worked to take the car apart piece by piece and now she scattered the engine, the steering wheel, the tires, all over the land.

Just outside his door, the boy found the stick shift. He bent to pick it up, and as he stood he saw something else in the distance. Another part. And another. The fragments littered the earth and he collected them in his arms, following the trail into the woods where it turned dark. The boy held the stick shift in his hand, and put his right foot out as if to accelerate, only to find he wasn't going anywhere.

His heart oozed out of him. It lay beside him, throbbing, and the girl picked it up. She placed it in a box and sealed it shut, throwing away the key.

Now the boy had nothing but the girl, and she was happy. She had captured a boy who loved his car and she was certain they would live happily ever after. She kissed him, covering his mouth, not noticing his lips were dry and unyielding.

Her white gown flowed down her back and across the ballroom floor like water cascading down a great mountain. She wanted to dance long into the night, but the boy was weak and unwilling, for while he'd been strong, her drive, her determination for his love was stronger.

After the wedding she wanted to go places, but the boy never wanted to. He sat on the couch and stared at the television as if in a trance.

"Why don't we ever go places anymore?" she asked.

But the boy, out of gas, didn't even turn his head.

SHADOWS AND PARTIALLY
LIT FACES

Dylan Douglas set an alarm and closed the door to his jewelry store. He turned the lock, placed the single key in his suit pocket, and heading downtown, maneuvered over the congested sidewalk like a downhill skier on a slalom course. He believed it was important to keep a brisk pace and professed on more than one occasion how this principle enabled him to cover more territory. "I do more, I see more. It's only logical," he said. "I live the equivalent of two lives."

Dylan reached for his cell phone and found the battery was dead. Annoyed, he scanned the street corners ahead of him for a pay phone. He spotted one and cringed at the thought of using it, detesting public services like buses, trains, and post offices, partially because he was unwilling to wait in line, but mostly because they made him feel ordinary. If he were going to be in a crowd, it would be at an elite bar uptown or a new restaurant in SoHo that required reservations weeks, if not months, in advance. He believed in living amongst the pretty people, and so he did.

The summer heat felt oppressive, the air dense. Two yellow cabs blocked the intersection just a few feet away, and the gridlock was causing tremendous commotion. Dylan knew after twelve years of marriage, he had to call his wife, even though he didn't want to. Callie would be angry that he hadn't reached out all day and that he wouldn't be home for dinner. Reluctantly, he stood behind a large woman with glasses and waited to use the pay phone. He wondered how this woman could walk around this way—messy hair, no makeup, overweight. Her brown leather sandals were stretched and worn, and he concluded that she was the kind of person who ate canned soups so thick you could eat them with a fork.

Now and again Dylan misread the signs, but for the most part he was an expert at sizing people up. He considered the customer he'd had that day. His father had taught him at sixteen how to distinguish between someone who wanted to browse and a real customer. Designer shoes and an expensive watch were solid clues. Dylan applied these criteria, both in his professional and personal life, and for the most part, he was right. In any case, he was right today, and he took a moment to pat himself on the back. When he deserved credit, Dylan made sure to give it to himself.

He reflected on how he'd been able to convince the man to buy his wife a diamond and emerald necklace. He told the man how women need jewelry this significant in order to feel loved, that bringing home something special for his wife was the right thing to do, and that he was sure she deserved the best. It would be inappropriate to go home with something small, or even, God forbid, nothing at all.

It was then that Dylan took out two crystal scotch glasses and offered the man a drink, Glenrothes, the best single malt scotch. He knew how important it was to charm his guest, and he was good at it, taking entertaining to new heights by studying fine wines, researching the best liquors, and cooking elaborate meals. He understood that to *break bread* with someone was to win their trust, their friendship, and he used this knowledge to his advantage. He assured the man that he would sell him the necklace for a good price because the man was a good man, and he felt like being a nice guy, too. By the time the man left his store, the two of them had smoked cigars, told dirty jokes, and drunk countless glasses of scotch together. Dylan had paid $12,000 for the necklace. He sold it for $38,000.

Still waiting to use the pay phone, Dylan stood closer to the woman, making his presence clear. He shifted his weight from one foot to the other, swaying like an impatient child, and thought about Callie and the fight they'd had that morning.

"I can't reach you," she'd said, her fingers clenched. "Even when you're home, it's as if you're not here." She crossed her arms in front of her chest, as if to protect herself from the fiery air between them.

He responded by ranting about how hard he worked, yelling until the veins in his neck protruded like squiggly blue lines on a road map. Her shoulders were pinned at attention, and he observed the fierce way she exhaled her thoughts, her needs, so that he did the opposite. He inhaled and held his breath until numb. He slammed the door behind him, frustrated that she was always trying to fix him, the way a mechanic changes an old tire that can't go the distance for a new one.

He picked his head up when he heard the telephone receiver being placed back in its cradle. The woman turned and quite unexpectedly peered at Dylan as if she were sizing him up, surmising that his hazel green eyes, his sharp-featured face, and his tall slender body were like a well-wrapped present; under the curled colored ribbon and the shiny wrapping paper there was always something you did not need or want.

The phone felt sticky as Dylan lifted it to his ear. While dialing his three-story, all brick, newly renovated house in Brooklyn, Dylan tried not to think about how he had overpaid for the house so he could live in the *right neighborhood.* He wanted the best for his family and the real estate agent had convinced him, *location, location, location.* As Dylan visualized Callie, the kids, and the frenzied chaotic behavior that went on at night behind closed doors, a harsh sound burst through the receiver, signaling that there was a problem with his connection. Dylan grimaced as he moved the telephone away from his ear. A recording began . . . *please hang up and dial again.*

Dylan slammed the receiver down, knowing what he was going to hear, something about using an AT&T operator. This wasn't the first time he had trouble getting through while trying to place a credit card call. He tried again, exerting great effort to remain calm, but he couldn't get a connection.

"Damn!" he shouted, crashing the telephone receiver into the chrome cradle that housed it. Over and over again he slammed the receiver down. He lifted it, and slammed it down again.

A young man on a bicycle with a manila envelope under his arm stood behind Dylan and waited to use the phone. Dylan needed a quarter, but he never kept loose coins in his pockets because they seemed to weigh him down, and the sound of them colliding was annoying.

It was getting late. Dylan took a deep breath, exhausted, and the air smelled of something gone bad. He pulled a wad of money out of his pocket, not noticing the boy's interest in the neatly folded cash. There was a single dollar on the outside. All the big bills were strategically kept on the inside. He tugged at the dollar, but was forced to slip off his gold money clip in order to retrieve it.

He turned to ask the young man, who was now straddling his bike with one knee up and the other leg down on the ground for balance, if he had change. The young man used his free arm to pull black headphones away from his head. Dylan could hear the beat of the music from where he stood.

The boy chewed gum and blew a pink bubble that covered most of his face. He brought the bubble back into his mouth, shook his head, and mumbled something about using the phone on the next block. Turning his bike around to leave, the boy spit his gum into the street with a propelled force.

Dylan was desperate for change and the effects of the scotch he'd had earlier were beginning to set in. His head ached in a dull but consistent way. He turned to a mother who was strolling her baby and asked her for change, knowing from experience that women with small children carried large bags filled with necessities ranging from diapers to Cheerios.

The young mother dug her hand into her bag and told him she knew exactly how he felt; she often found herself in the same situation. She went on to explain how she was sure she had change, she just wasn't sure which compartment it was in. She continued her search with deliberate slow movements while Dylan sighed and shifted his weight to his other leg. She smiled and pulled three quarters from the inside pocket of her bag how a magician pulls a rabbit out of a hat.

Just then her baby started to cry and she was distracted. Dylan was irritated but familiar with this kind of detour, and as usual he was resentful about having to wait his turn. The woman wanted to find a fourth quarter but Dylan wouldn't wait. He handed her a dollar in exchange for three quarters.

It was now dark and Dylan relied on the streetlights to see what he was doing. He dialed the number to his house again, even more anxious to get through. The phone rang six times before his daughter picked up.

"Hello."

"Hi, sweetie. It's me, Daddy."

"Oh, hi, Daddy. Where are you? I want you."

"I'm still at work, baby. What are you doing?"

"Playing."

"Playing what?"

"Barbie."

Dylan envisioned her among her community of Barbies, snapping their heads on and off their bodies one by one. "That sounds like fun." He paused. "Hey, sweetheart, you be a good girl. Sleep tight and and don't let the bedbugs bite."

"I'm not going to see you later? I want you to make dinner again like last night."

Dylan knew she loved it when he was home cooking, and he felt a stirring deep in his gut. Not allowing himself to focus, he quickly pushed the feeling away.

"No, sweetie. I have to work late. Let me talk to your mother."

"Mom. Daddy's on the phone," she screamed, not

knowing to move the receiver away from her mouth as she bellowed this information, and once again Dylan was forced to move the phone away from his ear.

"Hello," Callie said.

"Hi, babe, it's me."

A moment passed before she asked, "Where are you?" and he could tell she was still upset.

"I'm at a pay phone. On my way to Top Bar, that new place that just opened on Twenty-First. I made a sale tonight," he tried to explain. "It was a big one," he added for credibility.

Dylan heard the sound of water running and could picture his wife on her knees, leaning over the bathtub, holding the phone tightly between her ear and her shoulder, arms free as she tended to their children.

"I could really use your help here tonight," Callie said. "The kids are giving me a hard time. First none of them wanted to take a bath, now I can't get them out. Besides, I thought we could talk about what happened this morning."

"I need to relax a little. I had a long day. I'm just going to get a drink."

"You mean another drink," she responded flatly.

"I had one drink with this guy. He was a good customer."

"How many drinks?" she asked.

"One," he said firmly, and then softening, "Oh come on. I can't stand when you do this. I'm telling you I . . ."

The sound of a coin dropping inside the telephone interrupted their conversation. A recording of an operator told them that their time had run out and that the caller would have to put in an additional ten cents. Dylan was thankful for the break.

"We're going to get cut off. I have to go."

"You always have to go."

"I'll be home soon." And before he could say goodbye, they were disconnected.

Dylan sat at the crowded bar on Twenty-First and ordered Glenrothes. After taking his first sip, he exhaled and focused on the warm liquid burning through his insides. He thought about his wife and the conversation they'd just had. He wanted to go home. He wanted to be there, to help with the kids, to kiss them before bedtime—but he couldn't. Sometimes he just couldn't.

And then there were the times that he needed to go home, like a marathon runner after a big race. He would open the front door to his house, and announce, "I'm home!" It wouldn't be long before his children came running into his arms. These were priceless moments, and he knew to be thankful for them. His wife used to greet him with a kiss at the door as well, and Dylan couldn't remember when that stopped.

Finishing off his drink, he thought back to the night before, how he'd rushed upstairs when he first got home from work to take off his suit and tie, how he'd changed into navy sweatpants, a faded Rolling Stones T-shirt, and the slippers his high school friend, Marisa, had gotten him for his birthday, before he went down to the kitchen. Dylan liked his kitchen not because of the mahogany cabinetry, the granite floor, the granite countertop, or the granite backsplash, but because he was comfortable, completely at ease, and in control in that space.

The kitchen was organized to his liking: spices in tall matching jars, lined up in alphabetical order, on a shallow shelf like soldiers in arms waiting to perform their duty.

And it was only in his kitchen that Dylan allowed himself to explore, savoring textures, smells, and tastes, senses he usually ignored.

There were no problems in Dylan's kitchen. The only difficulty that presented itself was that it was a kosher kitchen—no meat and dairy products together, no shell-fish, and no pork. This was limiting but not detrimental. According to Dylan, life was full of limitations, but he was trained to have a positive attitude, to look on the bright side, and to see the glass half full. In following these principles, he'd learned to ignore the parts of his life that weren't working, for he was taught that these very limitations were actually blessings.

After all, he was a rich man now. It would be point-less to dwell on the fact that he had begun to work when he was only sixteen, never finishing high school. He'd worked hard for six years, never doing what other boys his age did before he met Callie, fell madly in love, and married her. They slept together for the first time on their honeymoon, and within two years their first child, David, was born. Dylan had three children before he was thirty, and all the while his parents, his relatives, and the neighbors smiled and congratulated him as he conducted himself as he should according to Jewish law and tradi-tion. There were many obstacles along the way—hard times with Callie, adjusting to the children being born, stresses at work—but he always figured out how to make it look good on the outside. Nobody knew what he really felt or what he really wanted, not his mother, not his wife, not his friends, not even himself. But in his kitchen, Dylan could present something that looked impressive on the outside and was genuinely satisfying within.

In the beginning, his cooking was more like a labora-
tory experiment than food preparation, but Callie was
supportive nonetheless. They laughed together on more
than one occasion as he encouraged her to taste what
he'd prepared. When he got good, Dylan began to invite
other couples for dinner. Entertaining was his pleasure:
bottles of wine, exotic foods, and plenty of friends telling
him how wonderful the food was, how wonderful he was,
and how lucky Callie was to have such a man. Dylan
wondered about the deception. Did they know how much
was illusion? A public face, a masquerade hiding private
disappointment.

"How about another?" the bartender asked.

Dylan looked at his empty glass. "Sure," he said. And
the bartender put a new drink down in front of him. Dylan often joked with his friends that if he could shoot
scotch directly into his veins, he would. He began to
breathe more evenly, one long breath in and one long
breath out.

Drumming his long fingers on the top of the bar, Dylan
looked around and noticed all the beautiful people and the
dark appealing atmosphere that surrounded him: red velvet
couches, small round tables with candles that partially lit
interesting faces moving in conversation, and the long,
sleek bar held candelabras, creating shadows that mesmerized him.

In a trance, Dylan recalled a certain day when he was
about eight years old. He had come home from a birthday
party to his impeccably decorated house, to his perfectly
put-together mother. She was standing at the door waiting
to greet him. As she opened the door, she smiled broadly,
all her gleaming white teeth showing, her arms out-

stretched and welcoming. "How was the party?" she asked jubilantly. Dylan had sat alone at the party, isolated and afraid. The group of boys at the party were like a tribe, participating, laughing, and playing. He was not sure how to belong there.

As he stepped inside, his mother closed the door behind him. He didn't have the heart to tell her he had not had fun. She had never told him how important it was for her that he belong, but he knew. He knew somewhere deep inside that if he did not have a good time at the party it would crush her, and so he lied.

A woman in a short black dress with a revealing neckline interrupted his dream-like state. She asked him to pass her a candle from the bar so she could light her cigarette. Dylan lit it for her and noticed the shadows on her face. He thought she looked good, although she wasn't particularly beautiful. There was a difference.

It wasn't long before Dylan bought her a drink. He impressed her. She had already commented on his suit, his watch, and his good looks. He knew from experience he could have her. It would be quick and easy, the way he liked it. He wanted to be with someone who he believed wouldn't judge him, wouldn't ask for more than he could give. If she did, it wouldn't matter, he'd be gone before she had a chance to complain.

As Dylan and the woman turned to leave the bar together, he noticed a crowd at the door, trying to get in, but crushed red velvet ropes made this a selective process. Waiting for his opportunity to move forward, he looked down and saw that at an intimate table for two a waiter had just served a salmon main course. Dylan observed the salmon dish closely, paying attention to every detail, specifically its presentation because he often gathered his menu ideas from restaurants. Peter and Dana, Eric and Marisa, and Howie and Lori were coming for dinner on Tuesday. He thought salmon with mustard and dill was a nice idea, and he wondered if Callie would like that.

He'd ask her in the morning.

LUCKY

Sally grasped Keith's hand as the plane moved down the runway.

He looked at her. "Are you OK?"

"I'm fine. Just a little nervous, that's all."

"We're going to have a great time. You'll see. Just the way it used to be."

Sally knew that was unlikely. But neither one of them said a word.

When the captain turned off the "fasten seat belt" sign, Sally got up to go to the bathroom. As she washed her hands, she caught a glimpse of herself in the mirror and didn't recognize the person looking back. She realized she hadn't looked at herself as an individual, a woman, in months. Her almond-shaped eyes, once dark as coal, appeared dull, and her skin sagged. Her lips, dry and cracking, hurt. She pulled her curly black hair, now streaked with lines of gray, off her face and secured the mass with a clip, forming a tight knot the size of a lemon at the back of her neck.

Her hair had been falling out for months, a normal symptom of stress, and she gathered the loose strands that were wrapped around her fingers. There was a time when this would've killed her, given how proud she was of its thickness. Now it seemed trivial. She searched her face, looking for something familiar but felt lost. She imagined that everyone who looked at her must see her pain, that they could actually read it like text, scribbled lines across her forehead, around her eyes, along her mouth, and down her neck. Engraved print that read, "My child is sick."

When she returned to her seat, Keith held the newspaper open wide. Sally stood next to him in the aisle and couldn't help but read the headline, "Couple Kills Their Three-Year-Old Daughter." With one finger Keith raised his glasses from his nose, looked up at her, and smiled. He folded the paper, making room for her. She forced a smile back and took her seat. Now and then her eyes wandered toward the paper, and she'd turn her head away, trying to avoid the story, but somehow she was drawn back, resolved to know the truth. The parents, she read, had scrubbed their baby with Brillo for urinating in her underpants. They nursed her wounds with a combination of alcohol and peroxide, and when she wouldn't stop howling, they drowned her in the bathtub, acknowledging that this time they'd gone too far. *Babies are like numbers on a roulette wheel*, Sally thought, *you never know which ones will be the lucky ones.*

Keith had always been a man of few words so, a year ago, when they got the news that their two-year-old son, Tyler, was sick with a rare genetic disease, Keith said nothing. He held Sally up as her legs crumbled beneath her. She grasped Keith's shoulders, the tips of her fingers white, and she sobbed into his chest.

The next morning, he still said nothing. Sally cried and clung to the frame of the bathroom door, and she watched as Keith stood facing the bathroom mirror. Bare-chested, he counted out loud the number of strokes of deodorant he applied to his underarms. He made sure to give each underarm exactly fifteen strokes. It had taken a while, but he'd done an experiment, he informed her. "That's how much it takes, fifteen strokes, no more and no less."

On the airplane, Sally stared at Keith as he read, and she could see her son in his fair-skinned face. She missed him already. While she wasn't particularly interested in traveling now, she knew Keith needed to get away. He'd been acting strangely lately, unpredictable, and out of character. Just the other night he jumped out from behind the side door as she carried a bag of groceries into their house.

"Boo," he yelped, lunging toward her.

Sally dropped the bag of groceries and screamed, "What are you doing? You scared me to death."

Keith laughed.

And recently, Sally had inadvertently left some dog food their dachshund hadn't finished in their backyard. When she realized, she went out to get it. Stumbling in the dark across the cracked cement, she spotted a rat eating the food, and she screamed.

Keith came running. "What's the matter?"

Sally pointed to the bowl in the distance. The rat scurried away dragging its thick tail, and Keith said, "Don't worry, I have a plan."

He set his alarm and, the next morning, woke up early. He went out and bought a trap. He set it and continued on with his day. The following morning, he was delighted to find a rat stuck to the bottom. "See, Sally," he said, holding up the trap, "you have nothing to worry about. I've got things under control."

He bought another trap and set it. The next morning, another rat was captured. Exuberant, he went out and came home with yet another trap.

"How long are you going to do this?" Sally inquired.

"As long as it takes."

"As long as what takes?"

"As long as it takes to get rid of our little problem," Keith said.

On the fifth morning, Sally went out to find Keith jumping up and down, high-fiving the air, and screaming, "I gotcha, buddy, you're finished! Don't mess with me, you hear?" and pointing his finger he yelled, "You thief!" Slowly he reiterated, one syllable at a time, "You are a thief!" And as he lifted the trap, his elbow bent, he looked at the rat in the eyes and said, "I'm sorry to have to do this, pal, but you can't come around here taking things that aren't yours."

A week went by before Sally convinced Keith that as long as he put food out, the rats would return, night after night. So, while going on a vacation and leaving her baby behind did not feel natural, Sally knew she had to for Keith's sake. After all, what felt natural anymore?

Sally had known something was wrong with Tyler almost from the beginning, but she lied to herself, ignoring the signs. A mother for only a few weeks, she propped pillows behind her in bed so she'd be comfortable as she nursed. Sally took in the heap of color in her room: a printed cotton blanket that housed the baby's playthings; books about numbers, colors, and the alphabet; toys that encouraged a child to reach, touch. She watched as her baby's mouth moved around her breast. Nursing wouldn't last for long, though. Tyler was jittery, uncomfortable. And intermittently, he'd pull his head back, stiff. She'd take her baby's hand in hers and kiss it, smell his palm, inhaling as if she could contain him in that breath, as if they could be one again. And then he would cry and pull away.

Up until then there were certain things Sally believed she could count on. In the same way that she'd been certain Keith would call every Wednesday night at eight o'clock to schedule a date for the weekend, and that he would wear khaki pants and a button-down shirt, she was also certain they would get married, buy a house together, and have at least one child. Silly of her, she now admitted, to assume that the child would be healthy or that you could count on anything.

Sally kicked off her shoes, reclined her seat, and buried her face in a pillow. Eyes closed, engulfed by darkness, as if sinking into the sea, she flew across the Atlantic, leaving her son further and further behind. And with that, she left behind her daily schedule of insurance phone calls, doctor's appointments, and therapy sessions.

"Mr. and Mrs. Rumson?" the flight attendant asked.

"Yes," Keith answered, resting the newspaper on his lap.

"I see here," she stared at a piece of paper in her hands, "you ordered vegetarian meals."

"Yes, we did," Keith said.

"Well, I'm very sorry for the inconvenience but we accidentally served your vegetarian meals to a couple named Remson in row eighteen."

"Well, get them back," Keith snapped.

Sally sat up and put her hand on his shoulder. "Honey, it's OK."

Keith jerked himself from her reach and said to both Sally and the flight attendant, "No, it's not."

"Sir, I'm really sorry. But there is nothing I can do. They have already begun to eat them."

"You expect us to fly for six hours with nothing to eat?"

"I would be happy to bring you something else."

"This is unacceptable." He turned to Sally.

"Keith, calm down. It's not like we're going to starve to death. They'll bring us something else."

"I don't want something else. I want what I asked for."

Keith settled down when the flight attendant came back with two garden salads and fusilli with tomato sauce. Sally was thankful the incident had passed, but she still felt uneasy. Unfamiliar with this kind of behavior, she wasn't sure what Keith was capable of anymore. When she finished eating she gave him a kiss on his cheek and told him she was going to rest.

Half asleep, she thought back to a time before she knew about Tyler. Now everything existed as the time before and the time after, two distinct spaces, separate entities, like heaven and hell.

Vaguely, she could remember herself, how she was then. Her garden—at the time—the essence of her. Sally was on her knees digging flower beds, a small shovel in her gloved hands, when the doorbell rang. She sprang to her feet, wiped the loose soil from her pants, and removed her garden gloves. Her small hands emerged white and stark next to the rest of her, protected from the burning sun, while her arms were dark, and she felt proud of her garden tan, proud of what her hands could create. Six months along in her pregnancy then, she felt proud of what her body could do. Her stomach swelled with life.

She looked through the peephole in her door and saw a UPS deliveryman. He was middle-aged and standing with a clipboard under his right arm. A small box rested in his hands. Sally opened the door.

"Hello," she said as she studied his legs. They stuck out from his brown shorts, narrow and long, incongruous to his belly, large and round.

Sally straightened herself, conscious of her appearance. She adjusted her V-neck T-shirt, tight over her newly swollen breasts, took a deep breath, and smelled the earth still on her. She reached for the package, anxious to see where it had come from. Smith and Hawken.

"Looks like my bulbs are here."

"You have a beautiful yard," he said. "You do that?"

Sally moved to the side, allowing him a better look. "Yes, I did."

"Wow, that's really nice." He handed her the clipboard. "Sign here."

"Thanks," Sally said. "Have a nice day," she added, before closing the door.

Cradling the package against her stomach, she carried it to the kitchen.

"You're finally here," she said out loud as she lifted the plastic bag out of the box. The bulbs were covered with mold, blue and spotted with disease.

"PASSENGERS, please put your seat backs forward and fasten your seat belts. We will be landing in Madrid shortly."

Sally lifted her head and rubbed her eyes. She turned from side to side, stretching her neck, and used the back of her hand to stroke her cheek, which felt hot and irritated from resting on it for so long.

The plane landed at 8:20 a.m. While they waited for their luggage to come around the carousel, two children stood in front of them. Sally assumed they were brothers.

She watched as the larger boy marched over to his younger brother and grabbed the bag that was in his hands. The younger boy attempted to retrieve it, but his older brother stood with the bag held high over his head, looking down at him, smirking.

"Give it to me!" the boy screamed, jumping up to reach it.

"Come on, get it," the older boy teased.

Sally wished her life could be so simple—she wished for what was irretrievable. The smaller boy began to cry, and Sally watched as his mother approached. Just as she was about to speak, Sally spotted Keith towering over the older boy.

"Are you kidding?" Keith asked, his lips tight, hardly moving. "You took his bag, didn't you?"

The boy didn't respond. He stood unmoving, staring at Keith.

"I saw you take it. You just walked up to him and grabbed it. I saw you." Spit flew from his mouth; his fists pounded the air. "You can't take things that aren't yours. Didn't anyone ever tell you that?" Keith turned to look at the boy's mother. "Didn't anyone ever teach him that?"

Sally hooked her arm through Keith's and pulled him away. "What are you doing?"

"What do you mean?"

"Keith, you're scaring me. You can't simply walk up to people you don't know and yell at them. What's the matter with you?"

"I don't know what you're talking about, Sally. I witnessed an injustice, so I got involved. What's the problem? I fixed it, didn't I?"

Sally thought she couldn't take any more. She had the

urge to run away, far and fast. Instead, she turned from Keith, swaddling her stomach.

She observed each piece of luggage as it cruised past her. A large black duffel bag journeyed around the bend, flowing as if on an electric river. Sally stared and wondered, who does that bag belong to? What kind of life does that person have? Do they have children? Are they lucky?

Keith collected their belongings. They went through customs and hopped in a cab.

When they arrived at the hotel Keith put his hand in his pocket to pay the driver and said to Sally, "Oh, no. I didn't exchange money. I only have dollars. I hope this guy isn't going to hassle me." He pulled a hundred-dollar bill from his wallet and leaned across the front seat to talk to the driver.

"*Señor*, excuse me." Keith showed the driver his American money.

"No, no," the driver said, wagging his finger at Keith as if he were a little boy who'd done something wrong.

"Oh, come on," Keith tried again. "It's *bien*. America."

"No. *No puedo, señor*," the driver said, and he turned his head away, pushing the money toward Keith.

"Hey, watch it. Don't push me."

The driver didn't respond.

Keith tapped the driver's shoulder, poking him repeatedly with his finger as if breaking ice with a pick.

"This guy's got to be kidding." He glanced at Sally. "He pushed me."

"For heaven's sake, Keith. He didn't push you. You can exchange money at the reception desk."

"He's just being difficult, Sally." As Keith stepped out

of the cab, he turned to the driver and added, "Go to hell, buddy."

His words, harsh and unexpected, gave Sally a jolt, and at that moment she wished she could exchange her life for someone else's as easily as one currency could be exchanged for another.

In their hotel room, Keith dropped coins from his pocket onto the white comforter, flipping them over, inspecting them one at a time: nickels, pennies, quarters, and dimes. "Did you know they all say, 'In God We Trust'? All of them. Every coin. Every bill. Did you know that?"

Sally stood at the closet hanging a shirt. "No, I didn't. I thought it was only on the bills."

"No. Look, it's here." He lifted a quarter, and then a dime, and then a penny, and as he pointed to each, he said, "'In God We Trust.' 'In God We Trust.' 'In God We Trust.'"

"OK, Keith, that's enough now. Let's unpack," and she walked over to him and scooped up the change from the bed.

Typically, Keith unpacked the way he packed. Shirts in neat piles, socks in rows, slacks hung evenly and organized by color. But not this time. Sally watched as he turned his luggage over onto their bed, scooped up the clothes, and sprinkled some of what he held in his arms into the top right-hand drawer. He used his foot to pull out the bottom drawer and dropped the rest of what he held in his arms into it.

After showering, they went back down to the lobby to talk to the concierge.

"*Habla ingles*?" Keith asked.

The concierge was a tall man who wore a black suit, a white shirt, and a bow tie.

"Yes, sir," he answered. "Please, how can I help you?" He moved his hands as if he were holding a tray of drinks he intended to serve.

"Well, we would like to make very special dinner plans this evening."

"Very well, sir. Would you like anything else? Tickets to a bullfight perhaps?"

Sally stepped in. "No, *gracias.*"

"Why not?" Keith interjected. "That sounds great!"

"No way, Keith. I'm not gonna be a part of that cruelty."

"Sally, I think you're overreacting. Everyone does it. We're in Madrid for God's sake. You know, when in Rome . . ."

"I know where we are, and I don't want to go. It's murder."

"What?"

"I don't want to watch some little man in tight leggings and a red cape prove his manliness by toying with a bull. He's a creation of God, Keith. How is teasing him with color and stabbing him repeatedly till he collapses entertaining?"

Keith didn't answer.

Sally rambled on, turning her back to the concierge. "Isn't life hard enough without causing deliberate suffering?" Sally looked away from Keith reddening and hoped he would drop this. She didn't want to be pressured anymore, but most of all she was surprised at his interest in seeing a bullfight. Since the rat incident, Keith seemed different, changed somehow. There was a time when they'd both agreed that to wear fur was animal cruelty.

"*Señora*, it is the tradition in Madrid. However, if you do not wish, we find something else. How about flamenco dancing?"

When Sally's childhood friend, Callie, had called to see how Tyler was doing, Sally told her that while she wasn't ready to leave Tyler, Keith needed to get away, and they were going to Madrid. Callie, having been to Spain, suggested flamenco dancing.

"OK," Sally agreed, and the concierge said he'd make the required reservations.

Sally took Keith's hand, and they turned to leave the hotel.

Hailing a cab, they headed to the finest shopping area in Madrid and entered the first café they found. They sat side by side on stools at a counter. A glass partition separated them from the displayed food, and they ordered using broken Spanish and pointing to what they wanted. Sally had *café con leche* and a tortilla. Keith had an espresso and Spanish *ventresca* tuna on toast with sliced grilled red peppers.

"Mmm." Sally licked her lips. "The food is always so good in Europe."

"This tuna is amazing," Keith said. "A piece of heaven right here on earth. After we eat, let's go buy some to take home." He studied the map the hotel concierge had given him. "*El Corte Ingles* is only a block away," he said, folding the map without following the creases. He shoved it in his pocket, leaving a huge bulge, and Sally cringed, noting this uncharacteristic behavior.

At *El Corte Ingles*, Keith went straight to the food department and asked the woman behind the counter if she spoke English.

"A little," a woman wearing a white hat and a white button-down coat answered.

"I'd like *ventresca* tuna, please."

"How many?" As she spoke, the woman's mouth moved as if she were blowing kisses, lips puckering to enunciate each syllable.

"All you have."

"Excuse me, *señor. Que dice?*"

"How many do you have?"

"*Tengo mucho. Mira.*" She pointed to a long wooden table stacked with cans.

"Ahh, wonderful," Keith exclaimed. He piled cans of imported tuna on the counter carelessly. Sally arranged them into tall neat stacks.

"Keith, that's a lot of tuna. We don't need this many."

"This is not about need. You can't find this at home."

The woman lifted her arms like wings as she pointed to each can and counted. "*Cincuenta y seis.*"

"How many?" Sally asked.

"Fifty-six. You have fifty-six cans." Again, she puckered, and her red lips framed her white, straight teeth.

"That's perfect," Keith said as he reached his hand into his back pocket and pulled out his American Express card.

"That's perfect?" Sally asked. "How is that perfect? How are you going to get this home?"

"Don't worry. I'll take care of it," Keith said, putting his arm around her.

The woman lined the cans in two shopping bags, looked at Keith, and said, "*Gracias.*"

Keith lifted the bags from the floor and lugged them to the street.

"Are you OK?" Sally asked. "Those look heavy."

"I'm fine," he said.

Just then Keith tripped on a crack in the sidewalk and stumbling, the shopping bags fell from his arms. The cans of tuna rolled into the street, and Keith scampered about, trying to retrieve them like a boy scooping up candy from a busted piñata. Attempting to gather too many at a time, they kept dropping.

"Look at this," he cried, showing Sally a dented can. "And this too. They're ruined."

"It's OK, honey." She helped him collect the cans, and with the two shopping bags back on his arms, they took a cab to the Museo Nacional Centro de Arte Reina Sofia.

The whitewashed walls of the museum were graced with grand paintings. Keith left the shopping bags with the coat check lady, and he and Sally strolled the hallways of the museum gazing at Picasso's work: a display of twisted figures, arms where a head should be, breasts too far apart, legs wrapped around a neck. While the parts were disjointed, tangled, or omitted, the image still appeared whole and intact. Like Tyler, Sally thought.

Her eyes scanned the edges of a painting, studying right up to the frame. You can't see beyond, she mused. Not further right or left. Just what the artist wants us to view. She was reminded of what Callie once told her about a person on a train who can only see what's in the window's frame as the train moves along. God, on the other hand, knows the bigger picture, and He can see beyond. This was supposed to be comforting somehow. Friends often tried to console her when she first got the news about Tyler. "If you're given a lemon," her friend Katy suggested, "you make lemonade."

THAT night at the flamenco club Sally and Keith sat at a cocktail table near the stage. Sally ordered a glass of red wine, her third, since she'd had two glasses with dinner, and watched as other tourists filled the room and took their seats.

The space went dark. A red light flashed and a full-bodied, big-breasted woman appeared center stage. Her ruffled, low-cut dress was red with black lace and draped to her knees. With closed eyes, she sang; words emerged from within her, exploding into the room, her voice rich with tradition and Spanish pride. White lights revealed four beautiful men, sculpted like the statues at the Museo Prado, standing behind her. They wore black tights and white ruffled button-down shirts, and they clapped their hands and stomped their feet like protesting children having a temper tantrum.

Sally took a sip of wine and threw her head back. Wine traveled through her body, numbing her fingertips and tingling her toes. Dizzy, she stared at this woman before her.

The woman's voice, so full of soul, reverberated. The long slits of her eyes, visible to Sally, teared. Sally knew enough Spanish to understand that she sang about the difficulty of lovers, you can't live with them and you can't live without them. *But what does she have to cry about? Robust, she probably carried her babies full term and delivered them healthy.* Sally thought about Tyler. How about the privilege to live at all? She had the urge to scream.

Sally glanced at Keith and wondered what he was thinking. What did he feel? Was this trip, this journey to Madrid, just another way to avoid his grief? It had been hard to face each other, the disappointment palpable.

They walked back to their hotel room arm in arm, stumbling over the cobblestoned streets, holding each other up. A light drizzle began, but neither of them seemed to notice or care. They walked on, the silence gathering like their pain.

It was Sally who heard the echoing whimper first. On the side of the road there was a dog. It had been hurt somehow, and it struggled to breathe. Sally bent over to get a closer look, but Keith pushed her back.

"What is going on in this world?" he screamed. The dog's stomach contracted heavily, its breathing exaggerated. Keith rested both of his hands on the dog's wet, bloody stomach.

"What should we do?" Sally sobbed.

Keith ran a hand from the top of the dog's head to his paw. It was raining harder now and it was difficult to see. He took his jacket off, wrapped the dog in it, and cradled the beautiful animal in his arms. Sally had never seen Keith do this with Tyler. He knew how to administer medicine and organize Tyler's complicated schedule, but he didn't know how to hug him.

The dog stopped breathing, and Keith screamed, "No! No! This can't be happening." He lay the dog back down on the street and blew air into its mouth. Using both hands, he massaged and then pounded the dog's chest.

"Keith," Sally cried. "What are you doing?" She placed her hand on his back.

"He needs air, Sally."

"Keith, stop."

"I can't give up now." He blew harder.

A crowd gathered. A policeman came to take the dog away, but when he tried to remove it from Keith's arms, Keith held tight.

The policeman wore a long black raincoat and stood with his arms outstretched. "*Señor, por favor.*"

For the first time, Sally saw tears collect in Keith's eyes. They dropped from his face, hit the street, and disappeared, like expectations. He let the dog go.

Sally wrapped her arms around Keith's waist, holding him up as if he were the injured one. He rested his head on her shoulder while the rain continued to fall.

"Are you all right, baby?" Sally asked.

"I have a headache."

"I have Advil back in our room," she said, facing him and rubbing his temples.

Still unable or unwilling to make love, they lay in bed together, melting into each other's arms, giving to each other what they could. Sally wondered if either of them would ever feel themselves again. Now there was nothing recognizable, everything foreign. The waves of blame seeped into the food they ate, entangled itself in their hotel sheets thousands of miles away from home, encroached on sleep, disrupted time and space.

Keith sat up and fixed the pillows behind him, his bare chest broad and strong. He turned on the lamp and reached for the map of the city of Madrid that was on his night table.

"What should we do tomorrow?" he asked Sally.

She sat up next to him. "I don't care."

"Me either." He crumpled the map up into a tight ball and held it high over his shoulder, like a basketball player. And he turned to see her. "What do you think?"

"You might make it."

"What do you mean, might?"

"I don't know. It is possible you could miss."

"I don't think so."

"Well, you could get lucky."

He threw the crumpled map across the room. It arched high in the air and hit the rim of the garbage can, then bounced off, landing on the floor.

"Almost!" Sally laughed, throwing her head back.

"You're laughing?" He reached for her, putting his large hands on either side of her waist. "I'll give you something to laugh about," he said, tickling her.

And they laughed together, surprised by the sound.

⸎ THE DEVIL MAKES THREE

It was getting late, and Iris still had a lot to do. She flossed and brushed her teeth, cut and filed her fingernails, and then she labored over her toes. She had to open almost every drawer in her bathroom before she found the Q-tips, which she dipped in baby oil, and cleaned first her belly button and then her nostrils.

Standing in front of the mirror looking at her entire body naked, she turned sideways, inspecting the folds in her stomach, pouch-like since having her sixth child. She pulled using both hands to spread the flesh, studying herself this way for a few seconds before she let go, knowing her stomach would never be that flat and unused again. Her breasts, once full, now seemed empty, and she cupped them, one in each hand, and lifted.

She removed her earrings and used a cotton ball with alcohol to sanitize her earlobes. She took off her eye makeup and separated each lash, scrubbed her face and neck, and got into the shower.

Iris washed her hair twice and did not use conditioner, adhering to the laws of family purity, the backbone of Judaic principle. She was taught that by following these rules, abstaining from your spouse for twelve days beginning with the onset of menstruation, not touching at all, a couple could achieve a higher degree of closeness on the night a woman was able to go to the *mikveh*, and the couple could be together. She had been told it should feel special, almost like a honeymoon each time. Iris wanted that.

She let her neck arch all the way back. Water rushed from the top of her head to her toes. She shaved her legs and underarms, scrubbed her body, and stepped out of the shower. Iris wrapped herself in a towel and used her open hand to clear away moisture on the mirror. She brushed her hair with a fine-tooth comb and removed the wet strands entangled around her fingers. Before she went out, she'd have to cover her hair, a declaration of moral limits. And once it was concealed under her wig or scarf, it wouldn't matter if she didn't wash her hair for a week, or two. Nobody would know.

She walked to her closet and stood staring at the selection of skirts that hung before her, scoffing at the monotony of her wardrobe. On her hands and knees, she felt around on the closet floor and retrieved a bag from the back. She double-checked to make sure the door to her bedroom was locked, opened the bag, and pulled out a brand-new pair of blue jeans.

Struggling to zip them, she pulled her stomach in tight, and let her towel fall to her ankles. Admiring herself in the full-length mirror, she turned from side to side.

The lever on her door moved and Iris froze as she heard the sound.

"Mom?"

"Who's there?" Iris unzipped the jeans.

"It's me. Can I come in?"

"Yeah." She stripped the jeans off her body and saw the lever on the door move again.

"It's locked," her son replied.

Iris stuffed the jeans into the shopping bag and threw the bag into the back of her closet.

"I'm coming, honey. Give me a minute." She lifted the towel to her and opened the door enough to see him.

"I'm bored," he said.

"I can't help you now, sweetie. I'm not dressed, and I have to go out for a while."

"It's not fair," he said, his head hung low. He turned and walked away.

It was moments like this when Iris wished they had a television. She could tell him to go watch a movie or cartoons like other six-year-olds. She could be like those moms who got a break, who used their televisions as babysitters. But according to her husband and the rabbis, the world was a corrupt place and as a result, they were forbidden to watch TV, go to the movies, or listen to music on the radio.

She closed her door and tossed a denim skirt on her bed, which was still separate from her husband's. For the last two weeks they'd been forbidden to sleep together, but tonight after she returned from the *mikveh* they'd unite. She got dressed and joined the two single mattresses, using king-size sheets, to make one.

"Sarah," Iris called. "Please come and read to Joseph. He needs to get ready for bed, and I have to go out."

Iris assumed that by now Sarah had learned about family purity at school and she probably knew where her mother was going. Iris wanted to talk to Sarah, to explain things to her, things a mother should tell a daughter, but more and more she realized she didn't know what to say.

As she moved down the steps, Iris tied a scarf around her wet head. Outside she shivered as she put her key in the ignition. She rubbed her hands together, covered her mouth, and blew warm air into them. Tucking them beneath her, she watched fumes rise from her car.

At the *mikveh*, in her private dressing room, spa-like and stocked like a shelf at Rite Aid, Iris flicked a switch, which lit a bulb outside of her room, signaling that she was ready. Impatiently, she waited, naked under her robe. She was cold, and her toes were turning a transparent shade of blue. She peeked outside the door to see if her light had gone on, to see if someone was coming, and she saw another woman across the hall who was also waiting her turn. Iris lowered her head and closed the door, respecting the woman's privacy. After a while a short, heavyset woman with yellow eyes appeared and with barely a "hello" she clasped Iris's hands in hers, checking for dirt beneath Iris's nails. She made sure there were no traces of nail polish accidentally left behind. Iris lifted one foot, and then the other, so the *mikveh* attendant could check her toes. The woman asked Iris if she'd flossed, brushed her teeth, and cleaned her eyes, ears, nose, and navel. When the woman was satisfied, she instructed Iris to follow her down the hall, where Iris took off her white robe and handed it to the woman, who would monitor her immersion in the pool of natural rainwater.

Iris descended the tile stairs, aware of the attendant behind her. She felt exposed, judged somehow. Burdened with the woman's stare, her eyes devouring, Iris never felt comfortable, and she wondered if anyone ever did. Stepping into the water always felt as though she was stepping into something biting, something with teeth. She dunked under the water, and, as she rose, she could hear the woman with yellow eyes call, "Kosher!" She shuddered, never getting used to this part.

When Iris returned from the *mikveh* her husband had already eaten dinner. He was in his study, involved with his books of Torah that were piled on his desk and displayed on the shelves all around him. His collection of books reminded her of when she and Morris were first married. She had been young and innocent, and she adored him, believing he knew everything. More importantly, she'd believed he knew more than she did. She leaned against the frame of the door and noticed that while it was almost ten o'clock he sat rigid, his white shirt still buttoned. His long neck was bent, and his beard appeared dark and coarse. Iris allowed this image to register before she announced, "I'm back." Peering over the top of his glasses, he nodded and lifted a finger indicating he needed a minute.

In her room, Iris got undressed. Morris entered without saying a word, closing the door behind him. He took off his clothes and slipped into their bed. Gazing into his eyes, Iris slid both of her hands through his hair, and then glanced down at her own body, an invitation. Morris leaned across Iris and turned off the lamp on her night table. Slowly, he lay on top of her. A sliver of light escaped from their bathroom, and Iris spotted the damage above. There was a problem with the roof, and the last time it rained, water had trickled through their bedroom ceiling. Iris could see herself up there, circling, as if she were outside of herself, separate and distant. She wondered if other women felt this way.

Iris tossed and turned all night and woke up with a sore throat. It was only six a.m. and still dark outside, but Morris was already gone. Every morning around five he left to pray and study at the synagogue. He went from there to work.

Iris felt weak and rested until one o'clock. Needing to do laundry, she climbed out of bed, wrapped herself in her terrycloth robe, and walked down the hall to her oldest son's room. Iris bent to pick up his dirty clothes that were scattered around the room and she put them in a pile. His closet doors were wide open and Iris felt a clenching in her stomach as she took in the sight of her son's wardrobe: a collection of white button-down shirts and black pants, lined up evenly across the rod. She swallowed, and it hurt.

Iris sat down at the computer they'd bought Joseph for his birthday. She pushed a button and turned it on. Having watched Joseph use the computer a number of times to study Torah, she knew what to do. She found the AOL icon and clicked twice.

The computer asked her to choose a screen name, and Iris loved the idea. She wanted to pick something exotic and out of the ordinary, but, fearful, she stuck with IRIS. Typing with one finger, she entered the letters to her name. But Iris was already taken, so she tried FLOWER, and that was also taken. Staying with the same idea but feeling limited and somewhat weighed down, she tried ROOTS, and it was accepted.

She was ecstatic when the computer asked her to pick a password, something she would never have to tell, her very own secret. The screen read, "Welcome Roots." Iris laughed and felt welcomed.

She spotted the word SHOP on the screen and clicked on it. Flashing on and off like blinking neon signs in Times Square were store names: GAP, Old Navy, Victoria's Secret. Fascinated, Iris paid attention, and the next time the words Victoria's Secret appeared, she was ready, and she clicked. Iris experimented until she figured out how to purchase a burgundy bra and panty set. She'd have to hide the undergarments, sure of what her husband would think of a woman who wore burgundy panties. Feeling giddy and a little brazen, Iris clicked the word PEOPLE on her screen. She saw FIND A CHAT, and clicked on it. Her entire screen filled up. Twenty-five people were online. She found their quick responses overwhelming and their names—Eagleeye123, Sexylady, and BigJoe—intimidating. She hadn't intended to go this far and all of a sudden, like a teenager breaking a rule, she was scared she'd get caught.

"Learn More about Yourself, Meet, Flirt, and Fall in Love with People Your Own Age," she read, stunned. "Connect with People Like You." She clicked on this phrase and within moments she was connected.

She stared at her screen, admiring its glimmering façade, absorbing the words, contrasting black marks against a white backdrop. Too overwhelmed to join in, she watched as others communicated. It was then that she received an instant message in the top left-hand corner of her screen. It was from H2O.

H2O: Hi.

Iris was nervous but decided to participate.

Roots: Hi.

H2O: Where are you from?

Iris felt a rush, a jittery tingle inside.
Roots: Brooklyn.

She hesitated for a moment before she hit the SEND button.

H2O: I live in New Orleans.

H2O: I'm a writer. How about you?

Iris was surprised by this information. She hadn't asked about a career. She recalled reading something about this, how people base who they are on what they do for a living. She felt cornered, not wanting to reveal too much about herself, intimidated by this person, a writer. She didn't know any writers. She only knew people who ran their own businesses, housewives, and rabbis. Feeling like she was playing a part, separate from her life, she typed:

Roots: I am a housewife. I have six children.

Iris wondered if this identified her.

H2O: Wow, six kids that's amazing. What an accomplishment.

Iris had never considered that an accomplishment before, and she found herself wondering.

Roots: Are you male or female?

H2O: Male. I am 42 and single.

Roots: Do you go online often?

H2O: Actually, yes. I go online to meet people, and sometimes I use what I've learned to develop characters for my writing.

Roots: Why did you write to me?

H2O: I like your screen name. How'd you pick it?

Iris hesitated, knowing she was crossing a line.

Still, she revealed that her name was Iris, that she'd wanted FLOWER, but when it was taken, she'd settled for ROOTS.

Roots: What about you? How'd you get H2O?

H2O: I wanted Water Bearer, the symbol for Aquarius, and ended up with H2O.

Roots: You're an Aquarius?

H2O: Yes, an Aquarian, a great talker—energized by ideas. A people lover.

A people lover. Iris looked at the words on the screen. Was she a people lover? Did she feel energized by ideas?

Roots: Tell me more about yourself.

H2O: Writing is my life. I also like to paint and sculpt. I enjoy good wine, good friends, and music— jazz and the blues. I love the movies!

Roots: What's your favorite movie?

H2O: It's hard to choose. My favorites are the stories that speak to me, guide me. What about you? What's your favorite movie?

This was the part that Iris detested. This was the reason she couldn't meet new people. It was impossible to explain herself, her community. She usually preferred to stay away, keep her life private. But because of the distance between her and H2O, two strangers separated by thousands of miles and protected by their computer screens, anonymous, she felt she could be honest and she wanted to explain.

Roots: I don't go to the movies. Movies romanticize love and life. They make you want things you can't have.

H2O: Stories express some individual point of view, an idea. How can that be bad?

Roots: It can be dangerous.

H2O: People need stories.

Roots: I have the Torah.

H2O: Oh, you're Jewish.

Again, Iris felt the divide. She looked at her watch and realized her children would be coming home soon.

Roots: It was nice talking to you but I have to go. My kids will be home soon.

H2O: I'd like to talk again.

Iris wondered if H2O was flirting. She signed off and massaged her neck with both hands, remembering that her throat was hurting. She had no voice, yet her fingers had danced across the keyboard, creating sound and language.

Just as she turned to leave, she heard a noise in the hall. Frantic, she checked that there were no visible signs of her activities.

"Hi, Mom. What are you doing in my room?"

Iris panicked, not sure what to say. "Cleaning up." She walked over to the pile of clothes on his floor and bent to pick them up. "You're home early."

"Yeah, my last class was canceled. Why are you still in a robe?"

It appeared to Iris that her son was studying her, and she wondered if he knew she had lied.

"I don't feel well, I've been home all day."

"Wow! You must really be sick. No wonder you're cleaning my room. You couldn't stand it, doing nothing all day, huh?"

Relieved that the tense moment had passed, she answered, "Yep, you know me, have to stay busy. Come downstairs, I'll make you something to eat."

Iris got dressed, headed to the kitchen, and began dinner. While she worked, she thought about what she'd done that day and she smiled, exhilarated and shaken up somehow.

As Iris put a tray of vegetables in the oven to broil, she recalled the night before in her bedroom. She'd been taught that sex was an important ingredient in a marriage, necessary and beautiful, a spiritual and physical bonding. She was a religious woman married to a pious man, a wife and a mother, and yet she'd engaged in conversation with another man, a stranger, something most of the people she knew would consider unethical behavior, shameful. But Iris wasn't sure what she thought. She hadn't done anything specifically wrong or broken any law. It occurred to her that she didn't even know H2O's real name, and she wanted to know more about this man, intrigued by his job and his hobbies; she would contact him tomorrow. She had a lot of questions she wanted to ask him.

The next morning Iris woke and glanced at the empty space next to her. She reached for her robe and searched for her slippers, spotting one under her bed. After looking all over her room for the other one, she gave up, annoyed with herself for not being able to find it. She put on socks instead and covered her hair with a scarf before she headed downstairs.

"Rachel, Rivkah," she called. "Your breakfast is just about done." She placed six plates on the kitchen table. Waffles popped from the toaster.

Sarah traipsed by, her hair thick and dark like her own, and Iris was taken by her beauty. As she poured orange juice into six glasses, she remembered how when Sarah was small, people would stop her in the park, at the butcher, in the grocery store, and at the mall, to comment on her mane of curls.

"Magnificent," every young mother remarked. "Just beautiful," every grandmother noted. But Minnie Mouse at Disney World raved, unsurpassed, with both gloved hands on her smiling cheeks. She'd waved her head from side to side, euphoric as she stroked Sarah's curls, and Sarah stared into Minnie's eyes and beamed, her dimples deep. After that, Sarah didn't complain when Iris wanted to brush out her knots. She'd stand still, gazing at herself in the mirror, unaware that one day it would be her obligation to cover what she now felt so proud of.

"Mom," Isaac said. "I'll have a bagel."

"OK, coming right up. Butter or cream cheese?"

Iris served them breakfast and prepared their lunches. She checked the clock and announced, "You're going to be late for school. Get going." All of her children were gone by 7:10, and Iris was alone.

It was an hour earlier in New Orleans. Iris needed to keep herself busy for a while, but she was good at that. *Distractions*, Iris thought, *are what I do best.* She got dressed and went to the cleaners, the grocery store, and the butcher. As she unpacked her groceries at home, she thought about going online again and speculated about what a man who cherished words, who braided meaning and language for a living, a man who found wisdom in some ideas and questioned others, might think about a woman like her: a woman who had a hard time deciding what to make for dinner or what color nail polish to choose for her manicure.

At noon Iris sat at the computer. She hesitated for a moment. But when she finally connected with H2O she felt satisfied inside.

Roots: I don't even know your real name.

H2O: It's John. I thought about you last night.

Iris felt uncomfortable with this, but she had thought about him, too, and before she could really digest this he added:

H2O: I thought about some of the things you said.
Tell me more.

Roots: What do you want to know?

H2O: Tell me more about yourself. I'm fascinated.

Roots: Why, so you can use me in your writing? So I can become a character, someone outrageous and foreign?

H2O: That's not what I meant.

Roots: What did you mean?

H2O: I never considered a movie dangerous before. I've never been married, I don't have kids, and I

don't know much about the Jewish religion. I knew
a Jewish girl once. A long time ago. Callie. Her
name was Callie. But we lost touch.

Roots: It's hard for me.

H2O: What's hard for you?

*Roots: Opening up, talking about things I've never
discussed before. I feel judged.*

H2O: I'm not judging you.

Roots: It's just difficult because I feel so alone.

H2O: Married with 6 kids?

*Roots: Some of the loneliest people in the world are
married.*

H2O: See, now that's interesting.

*Roots: I feel so different. Different from you, my
community, my husband, even sometimes from my
own kids.*

The words—no, her thoughts—were tangled and
knotted when they appeared on her screen. She wasn't
even sure what she meant, but she pressed SEND, freeing
her feelings and allowing them to soar through cyber-
space, comfortable with the fact that it was like that now.

H2O: Different how?

*Roots: Well, different from you in that I'm Jewish,
married, and a mother. We are a traditional family.
I keep a kosher home, I cover my hair, and I only
wear skirts. I follow the laws of the Torah. I see you
sitting at your computer, wearing blue jeans, a T-*

shirt, and a plaid button-down shirt—open,
unbuttoned, casual. You have a cup of coffee on the
right, a dictionary on your left. Your desk is made
of wood and the Louisiana sun streams through
your open window. The outside air sweeps over you.

H2O: You're close.

Roots: You see, you have choices, I don't.

H2O: Of course, you have choices.

Roots: I don't.

H2O: You chose to have 6 kids.

Roots: G-d wanted me to have 6 kids. That is my
purpose, to procreate.

Iris could hear these words fresh, as if for the first
time, and she wondered what she really believed.
She typed faster, spitting out the words she had been
told over and over again since she could remember,
and added:

Roots: After all, you never know which child will be
the scholarly one, maybe even a rabbi.

Iris indulged in this conversation, weaving herself in
and out of wonder, struggling with right and wrong for
over an hour, learning about John, his work for an envi-
ronmental group, his travels, the people he'd met, the cul-
tures he'd studied.

Over the next few days, sometimes without thinking,
Iris would go to her son's computer and write to John,
needing him to pull her in, into a world that was foreign,
open, and accepting. She allowed herself to think of him

while she did carpool, during dinner, and as she got ready for bed.

One cold night while she was preparing dinner, Iris thought about John and the conversation they'd had that day. Alone in her kitchen, she cut vegetables on a cutting board and with each chop she felt strength and clarity. It was then that her husband entered, and everything that was clear became foggy. She looked up, startled, and the sharp blade cut into her finger. She dropped the knife on the cutting board and wrapped her finger quickly with a paper towel. Her husband came toward her.

"Are you OK?"

"I think the cut is pretty deep."

"Let me see."

Iris unwrapped her finger, exposing her wound.

"Wrap it up again, Iris. It should be all right. I'll get the Band-Aids."

Iris was due to go to the *mikveh* in two days but for now, she was *niddah*, impure, and she knew her husband wouldn't touch her. This hurt more than the cut did. She felt anger build inside her, resentment that he wouldn't touch her during childbirth either. Once a woman had a show of blood, whether from the beginnings of labor or menstruation, she was considered *niddah* and off limits to her husband. When the flow of blood stopped completely, she counted seven days. After sundown on the seventh night she was able to go to the *mikveh*. And only after that could she be with her husband, hold his hand, touch his face, share his bed. Iris fantasized about what John would do in this situation, and it made her feel better as her husband laid Band-Aids next to her on the counter.

When her children left for school the next morning,

Iris got dressed in a hurry, anxious to start her day. She reached into her purse and felt around for her car keys, but they weren't there. She checked the pockets to the coat she'd worn the day before and looked in every drawer in the kitchen, frustrated that she couldn't find them. Trying to remember where she'd left them, she retraced her steps, willful and focused, and finally found them buried under some papers on the kitchen counter.

Iris did some errands and when she returned home, she contacted John.

Roots: Did you know I never dated?

H2O: What do you mean?

Roots: My husband and I were set up. Three dates and we were engaged.

H2O: Why so fast?

Roots: My father insisted we get married quickly. He worried about me, caught me reading Vogue once. He told my mother and they worried together. When Morris came around they believed he was just the one to save me from my "evil ways." A marriage destined to reconcile tradition with modernity.

H2O: What do you think about that?

Iris remembered when Sarah was small and Morris took her for an ice cream cone. He didn't know that she'd had a turkey sandwich half an hour earlier. When Iris saw her daughter licking ice cream, she casually mentioned that Sarah had just eaten meat. Morris grabbed the cone away, and Sarah cried empty-handed on tippy-toes, watching her treat melt down the kitchen sink drain. Morris squatted beside his daughter and put his arm around her, trying to explain that it wasn't kosher.

"Morris, she's just a baby."

"She's got to learn," he stated, wiping his daughter's tears away with a paper towel.

"There are exceptions."

"Iris." He looked at her, their daughter between them. "Don't start this again."

Iris had responded with silence.

She thought about John's curiosity and decided that's what she liked most about him, his ability to question.

Roots: It's just that nothing that used to be familiar seems right anymore. And I can't tell Morris how I feel because he never struggles. He wouldn't understand. The Torah is his road map.

H2O: What's yours?

Iris stared at the computer screen. She used to wonder what a man who never married or had children could teach her, but now, she was attracted to John's utter lack of fear in expressing how he felt. Stitched with the language of the soul, his feelings, he knew what he wanted and he went after it. Maybe that's what connects people to each other, she thought. Underlying, they want—no, need—some part of the other. Iris felt understood. Maybe she needed to be known by somebody. And at forty, it was time to tell someone who she was, or who she wanted to be.

Roots: For example, I shouldn't be communicating with you.

H2O: *Why not? Is our communicating wrong?*

Roots: *It could lead to wrong.*

H2O: *But it hasn't.*

Roots: *It doesn't matter. That's not the point. The point is that the sages have crafted a social code for reducing temptation. A man and a woman cannot sit in a room alone together with the door closed, men and women do not dance together at a party, and even when a couple dates they go to public places like a hotel lobby in order to never be alone together. The rabbis believe that when a man and a woman are alone together, the devil makes three. Even when nothing happens, something happens. So we build fences around fences in order to avoid temptation or any wrongfulness.*

H2O: *I can understand why some of those things are avoided, I mean if you're going to play it really safe. But why is communicating with me wrong? We've never been alone together.*

Roots: *No, we haven't.*

On Sunday, it poured, and Iris was pleased to be home with her family. She decided to read, and as she entered her room she noticed the ceiling was leaking again. The damage appeared severe, and Iris was annoyed because she'd meant to call the roofer but hadn't gotten around to it. She ran down the hall for a bucket, positioned it under the leak, and stood still, listening. Drops of water tinkled as they hit the bottom of the bucket. Within moments, the sound stopped.

The sky darkened, and Iris turned on the lamp near her side of the bed. Drawn to the rain pounding against her window, she stood with both hands pressed against the glass.

Iris looked up and saw the cracks in her ceiling were larger now and water was beginning to gush through the openings, soaking her carpet and the quilts on the twin beds. She climbed on top of her bed and reached for the ceiling. She jumped and felt wetness. The ceiling had absorbed what it could. Standing on her bed, a captain steering her ship, she called Morris.

Iris could hear Morris talking from down the hall.

"Sarah, how could you? You know better," Morris reprimanded.

"It's no big deal, Dad. He's my friend."

Morris entered their room, looked up at the ceiling, and said, "Iris, Sarah was talking to a boy on the phone."

"Mom, he's my friend."

Morris marched into their bathroom and came back carrying a stack of towels. He spread them across their wet carpet and immediately they were soaked.

Iris lugged the bucket full of water toward the tub. Agitated thoughts that were housed and brewing sprang from her throat. "Why can't she talk to a boy?"

"Iris, what are you saying?"

Tired of drowning in his convictions, Iris faced Morris and the words emerged. "She needs to learn."

"Learn what? Contemporary values? She must remain separate; that is our way. There are rules. You have to stick to the rules," Morris said.

Iris gathered her courage, the weight of her words heavy like the bucket of water in her hands, and she confessed, "Well, maybe my rules are different from your rules."

"Iris," Morris snapped. "The rules," he continued, "are not optional."

"No," she settled, "but maybe they're pliable, subject to interpretation." She heaved a sigh and studied Morris's face. "I mean, what does God want?" Weary, she faced him, her feet rooted in her sopping carpet, grounded to her resolve. "We need to think, we need to think about the purpose of the rules."

Iris paraded past Morris and dumped the bucket of water into their tub. Seizing a glimpse of herself in their mirror, she liked what she saw, distinct and vibrant against the mosaic tiles. She turned, pivoting on one foot, and slipped on the wet bathroom floor.

"Ouch," Iris said, trying to catch her breath as she lay across the tiles.

Morris came running. "What's the matter?"

"I fell," she sobbed, her body aching.

"Are you all right?" He squatted next to her.

"Yeah, I'm OK." Iris struggled to get up.

Morris stood and, bending, planted one hand on his front leg, and held out his other hand toward her.

Iris looked up at Morris, confused. "I'm *niddah*."

"I know," he said, his arm extended. "But you're hurt."

She cupped his hand, anchored it in hers, and stood.

THE following Friday, instead of buying challah for the Sabbath meal, Iris chose to make it homemade. Kneading the dough, she pressed and pulled with her fingers, like a child with clay. She boiled a large pot of rice, grilled eggplant, and watched as the skin shriveled and became soft.

She seasoned two chickens and cubed potatoes, believing that each dish she prepared had some direct correlation to how much she loved her family. After she set the table, she covered the string beans with allspice and put the roast in to cook. The smells of the Friday night dinner filled her house, permeating the walls, the floors, and the furniture as if the meal itself were alive and had a soul. At sunset she lit her candles and the flames flickered, vibrant as truth.

On Sunday, Iris got up early. For so long, she'd wake without sound or light in her room, but now as spring approached she could hear birds singing outside.

She put on her robe and slippers, tied a scarf around her head, and went downstairs. After pouring herself a cup of tea, she opened her kitchen window. Sunshine spread across the wood floor and warm air seeped in. She loosened her scarf, allowing the sun's rays to touch the top of her head.

That night Iris prepared for the *mikveh* carefully, knowing in her heart what was right. She covered her wet hair with a scarf and was thankful that it was spring and warm outside.

When it was her turn to immerse in the rainwater at the *mikveh*, she prayed. Dunking, she spread her arms out wide, and as they glided through the water, the wetness rushed over her, around her, and through her. Her thoughts were sincere and focused. She saw her family, her husband, her children, and she wanted to go to them.

At home Iris dried her hair, and it flowed freely like the waters of a river around her shoulders. She put on her burgundy bra and panty set.

When her husband entered their room and saw her,

he smiled—so rare, Iris thought, that it transformed him into someone new. It exposed his white teeth, filled out his cheeks, and unveiled the dimples he'd given his children. Iris walked toward him, an almost-naked woman. She put both hands on his face, and holding him there, she asked him a question.

⌂ THAT'S HOW IT WAS
WITH HOWIE

H owie reached for the pack of Marlboros on his night table and lit up. He leaned back against his headboard and exhaled. Smoke billowed in front of him. It was already ten, and he was due to pick up his six-year-old daughter, Olivia, from his ex-wife's apartment in Manhattan. He knew he should call and inform Lori he was running behind schedule, but envisioning her rolling her eyes, he dreaded that. "You're late," she'd say, as if he didn't know. "Olivia's been waiting."

Howie reminded himself that he hadn't intended to be late. He also hadn't intended to be divorced. He never intended to drink too much or stay out too late either, and yet here he was on a Saturday morning, sporting a tremendous hangover, alone.

Howie touched the ashtray on his nightstand, and it slipped from his hand. He peered over the edge of his mattress to assess the damage, like someone staring into a bottomless pit. Cigarette butts and ashes littered the floor. He blew, scattering the mess.

He couldn't believe how Lori had ended up in Manhattan and how he was left behind in New Jersey. Originally, when they conceived Olivia, Lori was the one who wanted to live in the suburbs, believing that children had a right to play outside in their own backyards. But at some point, she craved the energy of city life and couldn't tolerate the solitude any longer. Howie knew it was really him she couldn't tolerate, but he didn't want to think about that. He took a drag. "Fuck her," he said out loud.

He threw the covers back, got rid of the cigarette, and hauled himself to the shower. He stood under the water, letting it get hot, and watched his skin turn red. He stepped out of the shower, wrapped a towel around his waist, and cleared a spot on the mirror with his fist. He slicked his hair back using gel, brushed his teeth, and leaned in to take a good look. "You're the asshole that was left," he said, jabbing his finger at the mirror. He shook his head. "I'm talking to myself. I can't believe I'm fuckin' talking to myself."

He walked to the window and stared at the hole in the ground. He'd intended to put a pool in, but it never got done. Howie was known to be a workaholic, and during his marriage, he'd rarely spent time at home. Lori was ruthless in her badgering. She'd said she didn't mind if he didn't want to be around all summer, but the least he could do was get the pool finished so she and Olivia could enjoy hot days together, and yet, over two years had gone by. Lori expressed her dissatisfaction along the way, and watched, from the kitchen window, as workers slowly dug up their yard. She paid attention as the green grass disappeared and the black hole got bigger. Then, one day, nobody showed up for work and everything just stopped. Their backyard, dangerous and off-limits, was protected by yellow tape and a temporary chain-link fence.

The irony was that Howie was a builder; that's what he did for a living. And he was good at it. He developed multiple properties simultaneously—some twenty stories high, some sprawling for acres. But he wouldn't take care of the pool.

One night, while he lay in bed, Lori yelled at him. "It's not the Empire State Building, for God's sake. What's taking you so long?"

All he wanted, he remembered, was to be left alone. And now, he was.

His eye caught the framed picture of Lori that sat on his dresser. He'd left it there because he'd hoped she'd be back, and up until that moment, he'd wanted her to know she was welcome. But now, enraged, he hurled her photo into the garbage can. "I don't need you."

He put on a white Lacoste shirt, khaki pants, and navy Tod's. He grabbed his car key, passed the kitchen, and did a double take, not believing what he saw: dried eggs stuck on a skillet, and on more than one plate, an uneaten bagel hardening with cream cheese, and red wineglasses half full. On the stove sat a mountain of pots encased with tomato sauce and oil from when he'd attempted to make pasta earlier in the week. Empty Campbell's Soup cans and a heap of bowls he'd used for cereal lined the counter. He didn't want his daughter to see this mess, but what could he do? He could hear Lori's voice as if she was standing right there, and a vision of her flashed before him. "Fuck you," he said, walking out to his car. "I'll clean it when I'm good and ready."

Howie revved the engine in his black Corvette and lit up. He wondered how it was that Lori always made him feel bad about himself. She had something to say about everything, even the car he drove. The night he brought it home, he was elated and couldn't wait to show it to her, but he was embittered when she freaked and asked when he planned to grow up and act his age.

He turned the volume on the radio up high, and as if he and Lori were still discussing his car, he said, "I'll drive what I fuckin' want." He glanced in the rearview mirror and peeled out of his driveway.

He stopped at Starbucks and stood in line. Impatient, his head ached, and he needed coffee badly. He looked around. People sat alone, at round tables, and sipped coffee. Some read the newspaper, but others stared off into space, seemingly content with lethargy. Maybe they were slow moving because it was Saturday, Howie thought, attempting to cut them some slack, but deep down he was certain laziness was embedded in their souls, and it bothered him. Worse than that, he couldn't imagine being in public alone. Didn't they have friends? Howie had never been one of those people who could be alone. His cell phone served as a constant companion.

He dialed Lori to tell her he was on his way and was relieved when he got her voicemail.

The cashier counted change from the register deliberately, and it was making Howie edgy. "What's the problem? This isn't brain surgery." At the sound of his voice, the woman in front of him turned around. Howie aimed his chin at the cashier and said, "This is the downfall of our country."

When he got to the front of the line he ordered black coffee. "The biggest you've got," he said, handing the cashier a five-dollar bill. Dying to get out of there, he added, "Keep the change."

∽

OUTSIDE, he rested his coffee cup on the roof of his car and lit a cigarette. Exhaling smoke, he reached for his cup and took a sip. "Ouch," he said loud enough for a woman stepping out of her gold Lexus to hear. "Hot," he said, hoping for compassion, but she turned her head and kept walking.

Howie drove fast and got into the city in record time, but before he parked, feeling jittery, he smoked another cigarette. If he had called Lori, she would've brought Olivia down, but Howie wanted to get Olivia himself so he could see their new home.

He knocked on their apartment door, and from where he stood in the hallway he heard Olivia running to open it. "Daddy," her voice tinkled as she jumped into his arms. Howie hadn't realized how much he'd missed her.

Lori didn't invite him in, but from the doorway he saw all he needed to see: blood-red roses bloomed in a crystal vase; the sun had replaced clouds and now shone brilliantly through floor-to-ceiling windows; coffee-table books were displayed and stacked in size order. In the corner, on the floor, there was a knapsack. And curiosity took hold.

"What's that for?" Howie asked casually as if Lori's answer didn't matter.

"I'm going away for the weekend."

"Where are you going?"

"Hiking."

"Hiking?" Howie's face reddened. He could feel the color like fire, traveling up his neck to his cheeks. The heat was overwhelming, but he tried to contain himself.

"Who are you going with?"

"A friend," Lori said, in a way that begged him not to interrogate her further.

Howie felt his heart pound against his chest. Lori was moving on. She was now a woman who hiked. He also happened to know, because Olivia had let it slip, that while Lori used to eat plain old scrambled eggs, she now shaved white truffles on top.

The Lori he knew used to get in bed at night and slip her feet between his thighs, her toes colder than either one of them believed was possible, and he'd arch his back as if in pain, letting out a playful scream, pretending that this was torture. But he treasured that he could provide for her in this way. He missed that.

The problem was he simply didn't know what Lori wanted. If he had, he might have given it to her. Every time he thought he was doing things right, she made sure to tell him how he wasn't. One night, they lay in bed in the dark, fighting, and discussing divorce. They'd just come home from Marissa and Eric's party where Howie had too much to drink. Lori had spent the night eyeing him, so furious she'd forgotten to eat, and she was starving.

"Should I get you something?" Howie asked, rolling toward her.

Lori cringed and moved away. "I don't understand. Just a second ago, you agreed that divorce was a great idea, and now you want to get me something to eat at midnight?"

She was right, Howie thought. She didn't understand that it was instinct for him to provide for her, protect her and Olivia. That came naturally. But she talked about being *present*, and emotionally available, and he didn't know what that meant. She said she wanted, no, needed, intimacy, and he argued that if sticking his finger down her throat while she held onto the toilet with both hands after drinking too much at Dylan and Callie's dinner party wasn't intimate, he didn't know what was.

Lori kneeled down and hugged Olivia. "I'll miss you, sweet pea."

Howie noticed how Lori's voice lilted, and he felt a pang of longing. He pulled a pack of cigarettes from his back pocket.

"Oh, no. Not in here," Lori said.

"Oh," Howie retaliated, ready to explode. "I wouldn't want to tarnish your precious paradise. Come on, Olivia. Let's get out of here."

With Olivia at his side, he exited the building. The sun shone brightly and he squinted, taking time to adjust to the light. Just weeks ago, he would've been playing golf. Now weekends were spent with his daughter.

He pulled her in close, kissed her head, and inhaled. She smelled like strawberry shampoo, and he thought there was no one more delicious in the world.

He threw her Hello Kitty knapsack into the trunk and opened the passenger side door. "After you, miss."

"Thank you kindly," Olivia said. She put her seat belt on and looked at him in the driver's seat. "You smoked."

"Me? Not me."

"I smell it, Daddy."

"Must've been somebody else."

"Cut it out, Daddy."

"OK. You caught me."

"You promised you'd quit."

"I tried, sweetie."

"You don't try, Daddy. You just do it."

"That's easy for you to say."

Howie intended to quit smoking. He'd tried numerous

times, only to fail. But most recently he'd joined Smoke Stoppers, and he liked Dr. Frank Stern's methods. "If you're undecided, you'll get nowhere," Dr. Frank said. "In order to move forward in your life, you must find the courage to change. You're not a victim. You have a choice."

Every day for two months, Howie woke and faced himself in the mirror. He chanted:

I hate cigarettes.

I quit.

I will never smoke again.

He liked the ritual and was beginning to believe in himself when Lori moved out, taking Olivia with her.

"Promise me you'll stop, Daddy."

"I promise, sweetie."

They drove in silence, and Howie glanced at her. She was dressed in pink, and he was overcome by how small she was. From the day she was born, he'd loved her immediately. He recalled holding her in his arms, awed by her frailty, wanting to take care of her.

Howie stepped on the gas and zoomed into the Holland Tunnel. Olivia slid down low in her seat. "It's spooky in here. I hate it."

"You don't have any reason to be afraid."

"Yes, I do. What if it collapses?"

"It won't collapse."

"What if it floods?"

"It won't flood."

"What if we get trapped in here forever?"

"Olivia, stop it. Nothing bad is going to happen." He turned on the radio, and an announcer reported that a man in Monmouth County had been charged with sexually abusing children, using his job as a handyman to gain access into homes. Howie didn't want Olivia to hear the news so he shut it.

Olivia turned to him. "What was that about?"

"A bad man."

"What did he do?"

"He hurt children," Howie said, tentatively, not sure how much to tell her. He wanted to change the subject. It was making him angry. He thought of the children, innocent victims, and wanted to kill the guy who'd harmed them. He wondered how a grown man could mistreat a helpless child.

"Is he a daddy?"

"What makes you ask that?"

Olivia shrugged. "Just curious."

The car in front of them came to a stop. Howie hit the brakes and simultaneously swung his arm across Olivia's chest. "Sorry about that," he said. "Look at this traffic. Must've been an accident."

"Daddy?"

"Yes, sweetheart."

"I have to pee."

"Didn't you go before we left?"

"I forgot to."

"Well," Howie said, "you're going to have to wait."

"I can't. I really have to go."

"Olivia, stop it. There's nothing I can do."

Tears welled in Olivia's eyes. "I'm gonna pee."

"Don't you dare pee on my new seats."

"You only care about your car. You don't care about me."

"That's ridiculous. Of course, I care about you. Just because I don't want you to pee on my seats doesn't mean I don't care about you."

"Help, Daddy, really. I can't hold it in. I'm going to explode."

Howie looked around. He couldn't pull over. He couldn't move forward. He was stuck. He took a deep breath. "Olivia, you're a big girl."

She braced her hands on the dashboard, grasped the handle on the door, smacked at the roof. "Daddy, do something."

They inched forward. "Here." Howie said, handing her his empty coffee cup. "Pee in this."

"What? No."

"I won't look."

"I can't do it, Daddy. I can't."

"You can, sweetie. I'll help you."

Olivia took off her seat belt and then squatted. With one finger she pulled her panties to the side, and together they held the cup.

"Is it in the right place?"

"I don't know," Olivia cried.

Howie adjusted the cup, but Olivia moved it back. "What are you doing?"

"Trying to help."

"I can't do it," Olivia said, pushing the cup away.

"Look, we're moving," Howie said.

They came up behind a car that was stuck because of a flat tire. Hazard lights flickered on and off.

"Here's the problem," Howie said driving around the car and picking up speed. "It's behind us now."

Spotting a gas station, Howie pulled in and Olivia ran to the bathroom. Howie filled the tank with gas and bought Olivia a pack of gum. They got back in the car, and Howie stepped on the accelerator, heading south on the New Jersey Turnpike. When he reached ninety miles per hour, he whipped out a cigarette and lit it. He inhaled deeply.

Olivia turned to him. "What are you doing?"

"I'm smoking."

"But you promised."

"Listen, you. It's been a rough morning." Howie exhaled smoke and reassured himself that there was nothing more he could do.

ᕙ TICK TOCK

On the night of the breaking of the fast, as June's mother finished scrambling eggs in the kitchen, June sat at the dining room table and passed a platter of lox to her husband, Hal. Her father buttered pita toast, and her older sister, Lori, bit into a bagel with only a sliced tomato on top. Since her divorce, Lori had decided not to eat dairy products; they were fattening and bad for her heart. She became repulsed, and even went so far as to gag, every time she got a whiff of melted butter or cheese. Foods she'd loved her entire life disappeared instantly from her repertoire: no more bagels with cream cheese, pizza, baked ziti, eggplant parmigiana, or ice cream.

While Lori was considered eccentric in their family, June, who refused to dry-clean her clothes, smell wet paint or new carpeting, own a microwave, or use a cell phone for fear of dying, held the family title for most neurotic.

June took the platter of eggs from her mother and scooped some onto her plate. She felt a strange sensation throughout her body, and excused herself.

In the bathroom, a lifeless blob exited her body and floated in the toilet water. She tried desperately to discern one body part from another but couldn't, and was mesmerized by how uncanny and yet remarkable it was that the silhouette resembled a bean. She eyed it intently for a long time, trying to distinguish if it looked more like a red bean or a black bean. There was a difference.

When she couldn't make up her mind, she settled for simply being grateful that her child had passed naturally and, more importantly, as she'd planned. This miscarriage wasn't a surprise. She'd known for two days since leaving her doctor's office. *This kind of thing happens all the time,* she assured herself. *I'll try again.* She flushed and returned to the table.

The next day she went to the grocery store. She bought a variety of organic fruits and vegetables, organic milk and eggs, a free-range organic chicken, and every Seventh Generation cleaning product available, believing what was printed on the labels: "In every deliberation, we must consider the impact of our decisions on the next seven generations."

At home, sticking to family policy, June removed her shoes at the front door before she carried the groceries to the kitchen. She sautéed onions for a new potato recipe and chopped a salad. She gave her children, Ivy and Bea, ages six and three respectively, a bath, and allowed them to play in the tub with their new bath puppets while she sat cross-legged on the bath mat and read *Bon Appétit.*

Hal came home at seven thirty, as he always did. He read the girls a bedtime story and by eight, as was the routine, the kids were in bed. It was as if nothing had changed.

Three days later June developed symptoms. When she couldn't get out of bed, she called her doctor, who diagnosed her over the phone, informing her she had a urinary tract infection due to the miscarriage. June hadn't taken an antibiotic in over ten years, but her doctor scared her into believing she didn't have a choice. June, feeling weak, acquiesced.

She took Cipro, and when her symptoms got worse, her doctor doubled her dose. Two weeks later, when June still couldn't get out of bed, she read about Cipro on the Internet, and learned that it was like using a hand grenade to kill a cockroach. Cipro had side effects, some of them lifelong, and she discovered it could cause leg pain, loss of appetite, anxiety, flu-like symptoms, nightmares, sleeplessness, lack of energy, and depression.

"You're not sick because of Cipro. You have the flu," Lori said, intimating that June was overreacting, obsessing, as usual.

"It's not that," June said. "I know what I'm talking about."

When June still couldn't eat, her doctor took a blood count, checked for mono, HIV, Epstein-Barr, leukemia, multiple sclerosis, Lyme disease, and meningitis. All the test results came back negative.

"According to these findings, you're healthy as a horse," her doctor said.

But June knew better, and she also knew time was of the essence. She searched the Internet, addictively looking for answers, becoming her own doctor. She did nothing else; she wouldn't read unless what she read related to finding health. She couldn't cook or clean or watch TV. No other topic was up for conversation, and she thought obsessively about her illness, as if recovery correlated exclusively to how much she focused on it.

"You're making yourself crazy," Hal said, shoving Mr. Potato Head pieces back into the box.

"What do you want me to do, Hal? I can't move."

Over the next few weeks, June saw a gastroenterologist, a cardiologist, a gynecologist, a neurologist, an infectious disease specialist, a psychiatrist, an herbalist, a chiropractor, a kinesiologist, and a rabbi. She had a colonoscopy, an EKG, and an endoscopy. She went for acupuncture, reflexology, massage therapy, and iridology. She tried EFT, HBOT, and Reiki. She was diagnosed with fibromyalgia, rheumatoid arthritis, and lupus. She was barely able to walk, so getting from her bed to the bathroom was a production. Sometimes it was easier to crawl.

"Leg pain is a symptom of depression," Lori said, sitting at the edge of June's bed, visiting. Newly single, Lori had on a full face of makeup and when she stood in brand-new high heels, June saw that simple act as a tremendous feat, as if Lori had just trekked up the highest mountain, and June wondered if she'd ever be able to live life so simply again.

"I'm depressed *because* my legs hurt, not the other way around," June snapped.

As much as it killed her, June hired a housekeeper, named Bertha, who took over, feeding and bathing Ivy and Bea. Bertha read to them—*Chicken Little, The Carrot Seed, The Little Engine That Could*—and from down the hall, June heard them laughing. When she didn't have the strength to go see Bea dressed as a tomato in her preschool play, Bea asked her father why Mommy didn't love her anymore, and June cried.

Lori thought June's symptoms had to do with the trauma of losing her baby: postpartum blues. "Chronic fatigue," Hal guessed. June's mother thought the problem was mental and blamed June's predicament on June's father and the fact that there was emotional instability, even insanity, in his family.

Looking for support, June went to see her obstetrician. He put his arm around her like a patronizing father and, missing the point, assured her that she had nothing to worry about, that she'd get pregnant again.

But by then, June couldn't fathom having a baby. As her health was stripped from her, so was her desire to parent for she was keenly aware of the fact that she couldn't take care of the kids she already had. Her legs hurt more than she could express, one day tingling, one day numb, and joy these days was marked by something entirely different than in the past. In the past joy would've come the night Ivy read her first book, or while watching Bea roll Play-Doh at the kitchen table, or during the hour before bedtime when she and Ivy and Bea blasted music—the coffee table their stage, an eggbeater their microphone—and danced wild and free, all three of them, waiting for Hal to come home. But these days joy was finding a failed meter outside her doctor's office so she wouldn't have to hobble back to her car, feeding the meter quarters.

Her only relief was in the tub; warm water soothed her aching body, temporarily washing away the pain.

"You're gonna be fine," Lori said. "The doctor, all the doctors, said there is nothing wrong with you."

June lay like a corpse, motionless in her bed. "I can't stand up."

"You're just sad," Lori insisted. "I don't blame you. If I'd lost a baby, I'd be sad too."

June was in constant pain, but this time the hurt didn't come from the aches in her legs, her back, or her stomach. This was a new pain stemming from anger and frustration, a realization that she was deteriorating, becoming invisible. She was voiceless and alone.

The leaves on the trees fell, and June still didn't know what was wrong with her. She held on to the frame of her window and stared out. "I'm dying," she said flatly.

Hal wasn't overly concerned, mostly because he wasn't the type to fret, but also because he believed Cipro was causing June to experience distorted thinking, and while he saw his wife going crazy, he thought this would pass, as would her sickness. Nonetheless, he dutifully reported this new development to June's parents.

"There she goes again," her father said.

"I'm worried," her mother said.

"Stop it," her father said, walking away. "She's thought she was dying since she was six years old."

June had always been obsessive—the focus often on her health—and this fact lessened her credibility. Her father blamed this whole ordeal on yeshiva, resentful that his wife had insisted June attend.

"They put the fear of God in you in those places," her father said. "They mess with your head."

From the time June was in kindergarten she'd known about sin and punishment, and was petrified. At school, the rabbi, as if he were God himself, warned her about the consequences of not observing Shabbat. Every Saturday throughout her childhood, as her parents got in their car and drove away as if they weren't being cursed, June was in a state of panic, unable to focus on anything else, barely able to catch her breath as she waited by the window, counting bricks on the neighbor's house, until they returned home safely. With each passing Saturday she became more and more convinced that something bad would happen to her, or her family, death always on her mind, always a possibility.

As a precaution, she attempted to control what she could, minimizing risk whenever possible. Hal knew June had a fear of flying, but for their honeymoon he convinced her to put that anxiety behind her. He planned two weeks in Saint Martin. June boarded the plane with a surgical mask on her face.

"Do you really need that?" Hal asked.

"I do. And if you were smart, you'd wear one, too."

"I don't think so."

"Suit yourself."

June proceeded to whip out a package of disinfectant wipes and used them to scrub her seat cushion, armrest, and tray table. She buckled her seat belt tightly across her lap, refused to use the bathroom, and thought nothing of hushing the passengers around her when the flight attendant demonstrated how to operate the life preserver. When the woman sitting in front of her wouldn't turn off her cell phone as the plane taxied down the runway, June snatched it from her hand and did it herself.

"Can't you relax?" Hal asked.

"I am relaxed," June said, carefully enunciating every syllable, but her words still sounded muffled through the blue surgical mask. After that Hal preferred to drive, keeping their trips simple and nearby: Connecticut, upstate New York, New Jersey, Pennsylvania.

June visited her doctor again for the tenth week in a row, and after examining her he sat her down in an oversized leather chair in his office.

"This has been going on for quite some time," her doctor said.

"Yes," June said, looking past him to the accolades behind his desk, "it has."

"You plan to make weekly visits here for the rest of your life?"

"No, that's not my plan."

"Let me ask you a simple question. How's your marriage?"

"Excuse me?"

"Well, it seems to me we tested every possible thing we could test. According to the results, you're fine. Maybe," he said, leaning across his desk toward her, "there is something at home you don't want to face?" He scribbled notes in a folder and handed her a prescription for Xanax.

Even Hal, who'd been more than patient up until then, was getting fed up.

"Then do something," June begged.

"What can I do?" He shrugged. "You'll figure it out. Just do it fast. This is costing us a fortune. Look at this," he said, flipping over a wicker basket, spewing dozens of bottles of pills across their bedroom floor. "And check this out," he said, holding a piece of paper. It was a form letter: Insurance Coverage Terminated.

By Chanukah, June was desperate and went to see a holistic MD who practiced both Eastern and Western medicine.

"Candida," she said. "You have candida."

"What's that?"

"Yeast. The antibiotic you took gave you yeast."

"Are you saying the medicine I took to make me well, made me sick?"

"You could say that."

And while June was miserable she'd taken the antibiotic, something completely against her nature, she was grateful for a diagnosis. After all these months, at least now she could make a plan and follow it.

She kept a strict diet. Sometimes it was easier not to eat at all. Rapidly she lost weight, weighing barely ninety pounds.

On her way to the bathroom one night, she passed a mirror and was shocked at her appearance; not recognizing herself, she sobbed. She was a skeleton, a collection of bones, and she was frightened. That night she dreamed of white yeast multiplying inside her, growing out of control, and taking over her body.

Snow covered the ground. "I can't live like this anymore. I want to die," she said to her mother the following morning.

June's mother and Lori rushed her to the psychiatric ward at New York Presbyterian. The man in charge of security behaved like a prison guard, his neck rippled and thick as a tree trunk. He confiscated June's belongings: her purse, coat, scarf. The hospital staff asked her to strip and, following strict hospital rules, insisted she give them her bra, worried she'd hang herself when left alone.

June was given a blue paper shirt and a pair of blue paper pants that would've been baggy on someone who weighed three hundred pounds, so June at ninety pounds appeared particularly pathetic. "I look like a blueberry," she said, feeling small and diminished.

June was questioned and observed for three hours in a cold white room with fluorescent lights. She was freezing, her only protection the thin blue paper outfit she wore. The hospital staff eventually confirmed June wouldn't kill herself. From what they could piece together, she was severely depressed but not suicidal. They dismissed her, allowing her to go home.

That night, after everyone fell asleep, Hal went to the kitchen to get a snack. A sliver of light shone across the kitchen floor, and he saw ants. He saw hundreds of them, maybe thousands, carrying giant crumbs on their backs, as if hauling heavy weight. Hal, furious because June refused to allow an exterminator to spray chemicals in their home, stepped on the ants at first here and there, one by one, but soon found himself in a tizzy, out of control, stomping with vigor, jumping up and down, killing them as if they were a great danger. When he saw more ants, clusters of them, traveling in the nooks and crannies of their kitchen, he reached for the hose on the sink and sprayed the floor, creating a sea of floating dead ants. "Here today, gone tomorrow," Hal said. And like a madman he aimed the hose as if it were a weapon. "Bull's-eye," he chanted, pulling the lever.

June heard the racket from her room and dragged herself to the stairs. She gripped the banister, fearful she'd fall, and screamed down, "Hal, what's going on down there?"

The sound of her voice jolted him and he shut the water. "Nothing, everything's fine," Hal said, cleaning up the mess.

Pain moved through June's body, slithering like a snake, creeping to her head, crawling up her legs, slinking inside her stomach. It was Passover when she told the holistic MD that the pain from her legs had moved, that now it was in her hands. The doctor looked at her as if she were a child, fibbing. "Now," he said, with a tinge of disgust, "you're being a hypochondriac."

June, furious, insisted on one more test.

"You were checked for Lyme disease back in October."

"Test me again."

This time the results were positive. June had Lyme disease. Livid that not one of her doctors had mentioned Lyme results could be falsely negative, and that she'd been ill unnecessarily for over a year, she called each one, gave them a piece of her mind, and then hung up, smashing the phone to the receiver before they could refute, defend, or apologize.

One doctor after another professed that Lyme disease was hard to get and easy to cure. Two to four weeks of antibiotics and you're done. Doctors claimed that when patients didn't recover within that time, they had some other ailment, not Lyme. But after a four-week course of oral antibiotics, June wasn't better. If she'd been diagnosed and treated earlier this might've been enough but at this stage, she knew it wasn't.

Her doctor said it would take time for her to get her strength back but that she no longer needed antibiotics. "In fact," he went on, "long-term antibiotic use is harmful to your health."

June, still not having the strength to stand, sat. "What could be more harmful to my health? Look at me."

She searched the Internet and found what was called a Lyme-literate doctor, a man who was in jeopardy of losing his medical license for unsafe medical practices. He'd been hauled to the medical review board a number of times because he persisted in treating patients aggressively with long-term intravenous antibiotics. That day, she had a PICC line put in.

She had her first Herxheimer reaction that night.

June was prepared for her body's response, knowing that a herx, or cleansing crisis, could get severe as the bacteria in her body died off, but Hal was unprepared. To him, it looked as if she wouldn't survive. She lay in bed, lights off, a washcloth covering her face. She couldn't speak and was in excruciating pain. At one point, she stopped breathing. Hal called 911.

"You're going to get worse before you get better," her doctor warned.

"I'm ready," June said, as if preparing for war. By the end of the week, after experiencing her third herx reaction—which looked like a full-fledged seizure—her family, once again became cynical, wondering why she had to be so extreme. But this was the fight of June's life, a battle against the bacteria in her body, her family, and the medical community.

After three months of intravenous antibiotics, and nearly a year and a half after she first felt sick, June had the PICC line taken out but continued with a strict regimen of supplements and maintained a limited diet in an attempt to rebuild her immune system and her life. Three times a week she injected herself twenty times, up and down her thighs at acupuncture points, with bee venom. It wasn't the life she'd imagined, but this was the life she got. Her body couldn't move as it once had when she'd wanted to be a ballerina. The dance she did wasn't on a stage; it was across the landscape of Lyme—a kick, a pivot, a leap over unfamiliar terrain. And while it had been the most horrific, lonely experience of her life, her recovery was a miracle.

On the last night of Chanukah, June fried potato latkes. Ivy and Bea played dreidel, and Hal tinkered with music. When June's favorite song came on, she shimmied her way to the den and, dancing to the music, thought about a baby that for so long she couldn't imagine having. She held her empty belly and quickly let it go. Her children watched, wide-eyed and smiling as she did a twirl, and then another, a curtsy, a bow, before strutting to the menorah, which sat like an anchor in their window. June stood with her arms around Ivy and Bea. Hal struck a match and they lit the candles. Nine bold flames reflected against the pane.

Ce DROWNING GIRL

'm standing in front of the bathroom mirror, using a wet
washcloth to scrub at a dark spot the size of a prune
near my mouth, but it won't come off. It's my own fault. I
wasn't paying attention. I didn't think I had to because
the doctor I went to was some kind of hot shot whose
office was on the Upper East Side, just off Fifth Avenue.
Oblivious, I reclined on her dermatologist chair, under a
glaring and, now that I think about it, daunting light,
telling her that she couldn't buy the dress I was wearing
because it was old and, anyway, I'd bought it in L.A.
That's when she shot me with Botox in my jaw when it
should've been in my forehead.

"Hey, what was that?" I said.

"You're going to love it. Trust me," she said.

I paid her $1,200 and left.

That was three days ago, and I'm so clueless about
what to do next it's as if my bare feet are glued to the
bathroom floor. From where I stand, I chuck the washcloth into the hamper and curse out loud because I have a
party to go to and I need to look my best. Alex, my
boyfriend, my so-called boyfriend, and boss, owns a
gallery, and the party is at this guy's house. A prominent
art collector. Chase Bentley.

Alex wants me to go with him because he wants
Chase to invest in a Warhol and he needs to be seen in a

certain light—as the kind of man who is relational, someone Chase can trust. Alex didn't say any of that to me.
But I know him. I know how he works. We've been together for years, me and Alex.

Looking in the mirror, I glare at the bruise—all black,
no blue—as if I can intimidate it into going away. I curse
again, but this time notice my mouth looks funny. So I
bring my face closer to the mirror to test things out, and
I'm certain my smile isn't right. It's terse and fake. It's a
sort of half smile, a fraction of my real smile, divided and
reduced like a math problem. That matters when, your
whole life, your smile has been your power. No, let's be
clear: my smile is my superpower. It's how I got my father to take me for ice cream and how I got the boys at a
party to ask me to dance.

There's nothing I can do. I mean, I can call my doctor
and explain—or well, yell—that the result is shocking,
and more importantly, not what I asked for, but I'll still
be left eyeing a stranger every time I look in the mirror—
an eerie reflection of a woman whose aura is as dead as
the muscles in her face. It's all so blatantly clear. I'm approaching fifty. And no longer a sunny beauty.

Don't get me wrong. I was never a supermodel or
anything. I was never like Michelle Pfeiffer or Farrah
Fawcett, although, God knows, I wanted to be. But youth
is youth, right? You can't argue. Tight, blemish-free skin
is more appealing than saggy, spotted skin.

I know, I know—I'm supposed to embrace every stage
of my life as if I were a magnificent caterpillar. I'm supposed to be grateful that I'm alive at all. But I have this
urge to wear a sign, to scream from rooftops—

I WAS ONCE YOUNG AND PRETTY.

THIS, WHO YOU SEE NOW, IS NOT ME.

You don't get empathy for that. In fact, you get shamed for not being appreciative of every blessed stage of your glorious life. But something huge is gone. Lost forever. We should be allowed to grieve.

I keep looking in the mirror and trying to smile but it's no use, my mouth isn't working properly. My lips won't extend past the width of my nose, and I need to get moving or I'm going to be late for the party.

There's nothing I can do about my compromised smile but I can attempt to hide the bruise, so on the way up-town, I stop at Bloomingdale's to get my makeup done. A woman named Jasmine props me up on a high stool. She is dressed in all black and there is a tattoo of a willow tree on her bicep. A holster circles her waist. Lipstick tubes line the black leather like bullets. She studies my face and pinches the skin on my cheeks, seeing how it bounces back. She runs a finger over the dark bruise. "What happened?"

"I walked into a kitchen cabinet," I say, avoiding eye contact.

Jasmine gets to work on me as if I'm a slab of clay just waiting to be molded and she asks me about myself, and what I do for a living, while she cleanses my skin. She leans in and strokes a tissue along my face so softly, and with such care, I have to resist telling her I won't break. Instead I answer her questions. I tell her I work with an art curator named Alex. I tell her about Chase Bentley and how he lives in a townhouse, which is really a mansion, on East Sixty-Fourth Street, just off Madison. I tell her that's where I'm going after I get my makeup done, and that the women there will be gorgeous. They'll be five foot seven and taller. They'll weigh 110 pounds and less. They'll have arms with definition and they'll be wearing skirts so short you'd think they were sashes. The soles of their shoes will be red, the heels sharp as knives. But I keep to myself that these women will have flawless, pre-Botox skin, and not one of them will be hiding a bruise near her mouth, the consequence of chasing the impossible.

In the art world—OK, let's be honest, in every world —looks matter. Sometimes more than your résumé. When Alex and I work a deal, he's the front man, putting on a show, and I stand next to him, looking pretty—black Theory pants, a crisp white blouse, red Prada pumps. Some of the younger girls wear flats, but I can't. I just can't.

Jasmine's massaging my cheeks with cream. My shoulders settle down. My hands unclench, and in no time, I'm telling her how I worked under Alex for years before he made a move on me. I'm almost bragging when I say I didn't stand a chance; Alex was a big deal in the art world, and I was super impressed by him.

I find myself telling Jasmine that Alex is gorgeous, and rich, and it's so unfair how with each passing day he seems to get better looking, an Adonis with a sculpted physique, while my waist thickens no matter what I eat. Or don't eat. I exercise and eat blueberries, while he can gobble down a whole pizza right before bed. Alex has thick black hair with a few silver strands near his temples, just enough to illuminate his face.

I go on to tell Jasmine that Alex just turned fifty and I'm only a few months behind him. Over the years, when I've questioned if he's right for me, some Botoxed foreheads have actually managed to rise in bewilderment. My friends are always like, *Come on, Kelly, get real.* "I know what they think. They think I should thank my lucky stars he's with me at all, as if he's sticking by me through cancer, or something."

Jasmine tells me she's bi and that I have nice cheekbones.

I say thank you and try to smile.

Jasmine has short black hair and wears a tiny gold hoop in her nose, which I observe up close while she pats my face with a sponge.

"I won't be subjugated by men any longer. I'm done with that," Jasmine says. Her skin is dewy, *so, so* dewy it glistens like a tear. She has a tough-guy persona, adding something about needing to stand in her own power, and she has my undivided attention as she uses a Q-tip like a feather to clean smudged mascara from my lids. It's weird because there's nothing sexy about Jasmine, nothing sexy at all, which somehow makes her sexy.

"I'm an alpha female," Jasmine continues. This equates to something like ferocious lion, something to stay clear of, and I feel like a dying species. I don't tell Jasmine any more details about my relationship with Alex or how we became lovers, because I'm not in the mood to defend myself.

Jasmine informs me that my skin is dry. She applies serum with a cold fingertip as if it's a magic potion, as if she's Ponce de León himself, and the bottle contains the Fountain of Youth. She dabs sparingly and tells me I should be applying the serum twice a day and that the bottle costs $350. She says this as if it's no big deal, a bargain at the ninety-nine-cent store, and even though I know this is part of her job, I'm annoyed.

Still, she's nothing like the guy who, a week ago, lured me into his shop from off the street to sample a cream he swore obliterated wrinkles. Once he got me inside, he talked and talked, and I couldn't get a word in edgewise. I just listened, not wanting to be rude, and when I finally walked out close to an hour later, I was late for a meeting and $800 poorer.

"Close your eyes," Jasmine says, and I realize how tired I am.

The first night Alex and I slept together, we'd gone to an Italian restaurant on the Upper East Side, where an art collector signed a check for six digits on the spot, while we were still sitting at the bar. The sale was so easy, too easy. Alex and I felt like thieves. Bonnie and Clyde or something. Back at his apartment, we opened a bottle of wine. That wasn't unusual, I'd celebrated with him there before. But we downed two bottles, which was unusual. I was surprised when Alex leaned in to kiss me, so I hesitated for a moment, knowing I'd be making a cardinal error. I kept saying to myself, *You don't sleep with your boss. You don't. You just don't.*

But I did. And it was good. Really good. And I surrendered to the fantasy of Alex and me like someone slipping into something more comfortable. Everything was spectacular. Even his sheets were divine. I should know. I picked them. But it was something altogether different to be naked under them.

Jasmine tells me it's essential I use under-eye cream. With a tiny plastic spatula, she scoops out a smidgen and hands me a mirror so I can see how the cream works miracles, wiping away fine lines. "You have dark circles," Jasmine says, as if she's a doctor simply diagnosing, listing another symptom of a progressive disease. And it occurs to me that getting my makeup done has become as brutal as bathing suit shopping.

I stare at Jasmine's legs. I never used to, but now I stare at young girls' legs all the time. I watch as they cross the street in short skirts and flimsy cotton dresses. I'm jealous of their bare, shiny skin. The thought that keeps me going is that while they don't know what they have, they don't know what's coming. They don't know that one day all that beauty, all that perfectly taut skin, will be taken away. And just like anyone who loses anything—a puppy, a boyfriend, good health—they will be heartbroken. Jasmine hands me a mirror and I realize it's going to be impossible to get over the Botox debacle. I'm reminded of it every time I catch a glimpse of myself.

It seems to me there are two kinds of women in the world. Those with Botox and those without. The ones without judge those of us with. They want us to leave well enough alone. But I can't. If paint peels, I call a painter. And while there are twenty-seven-year-olds getting Botox, declaring preventative measures, there is a counter-movement going on as well—*Aging Is Wonderful.*

It irks me. It really does. It's disingenuous, if not full of outright lies. Everyone knows fresh flowers are better than week-old ones, and ripe fruit is better than overripe fruit—wrinkled and moments away from being tossed into a garbage can or blended into a smoothie.

Magazines feature models with Botox, airbrushed to perfection on one page, and on the adjacent page you'll see the latest politically correct deception:

Embrace Your Age and Conquer the World
Beautiful at Any Age

You're Only as Old as You Feel, So Let's Feel Good About It. Let's Even Brag About It.

Scientists have discovered that how you feel about aging matters—a lot. And my attitude sucks. But I can't help it because all the optimistic conversation around aging feel to me like "The Emperor's New Clothes." It's like trying to spin bouts of gas or bad breath into something desirable.

I want to boycott.

I want to picket.

But instead, I do the opposite.

I read more articles encouraging me to age gracefully.

I follow a slew of life coaches on Instagram.

I take deep breaths.

I practice positivity.

I say a daily mantra because according to Buddha, "The mind is everything and what you think you become." Petrified of that outcome, I look in the mirror first thing every morning and repeat ten times, "Kelly, you are beautiful just as you are."

Jasmine dabs concealer over my bruise. "There's a formula," she says. "Take your weight and divide by two. That's how many ounces of water you should drink every day."

"That's a lot of water," I say, picturing myself emailing JPEGs of art to collectors, writing news releases, answering phone calls, updating inventory, ordering lunch, applying for a booth at Art Basel Miami, and simultaneously chugging gallons of water. "That's not happening."

"Suit yourself," Jasmine shrugs, as if all she can do is prescribe. "Look down," she says, applying mascara with broad strokes. "You have nice lashes."

But given the bruise, the Botox, my dry skin, dark circles, and fine lines, my lashes feel like a consolation prize.

"Look up," Jasmine says. She brings her face close to mine and I can feel her light breath on my cheeks. Separating my lashes with a fingernail, she sticks out her tongue, concentrating. She squints, and I notice a groove down the middle of her forehead. I can't help it. I feel a tinge of satisfaction.

ALEX and I meet on the corner of Madison and Sixty-Fourth so we can walk into the party together. The first thing he says when he sees me is, "You look different." He's staring, scrutinizing me like a piece of art he's checking with blacklight. I turn away.

"Good," he says, still looking me up and down, "just different."

We enter the home of Chase Bentley, famous billionaire, and a butler in a black tuxedo takes our coats. The limestone foyer has low ceilings and the space feels tomb-like, airless and cold. Alex and I climb the winding marble staircase. Halfway up, Alex says, "Glad I decided on the penthouse."

For a solid two years, Alex studied the New York City real estate market, and visited every available luxury property. He considered a townhouse because he thought he'd have more space to display his art collection, but in the end, decided he was better off with an elevator, and not dealing with stairs every time he wanted something from the refrigerator. Plus, he needed services—a doorman and a concierge, people to do things for him like a wife.

At the top of the stairs, the Warhol I sent over on consignment hangs above the lit fireplace. It's the star of the show, the reason for the party. A bright light shines on the masterpiece, illuminating every detail.

I look around, taking in the regal home decor, rich tones of burgundy and gold. On this floor, the ceilings are fourteen feet high and there is a huge bay window overlooking an old, bare tree. It must be magnificent in the summertime, and the light, the natural light must be glorious. There are crown moldings and Gracie panels. Chase's home is old-world beautiful like a museum.

The house smells like pungent perfume and is crowded with stunning young women, imitation Gagosian girls with legs thin as black widow spiders. I spot Chase across the room. He lifts his arm over his head and waves, navigating through the crowd to greet us. He is wearing a charcoal cashmere suit, a crisp white shirt, and a navy tie. He says hello to Alex and shakes his hand, and kisses me twice, once on each cheek. A man wearing a black corduroy sports jacket, white sneakers, and a pink leather tie, someone I've never met before, puts his arm around Alex and steers him away.

Holding a scotch, Chase stands too close to me, and I smell alcohol on his breath. I stare at his hands, and his skin is blotchy as a week-old banana. He's around eighty and to him, I'm young. Maybe even beautiful. He's a flirt, the old-fashioned kind, from the Hugh Hefner era, and he hasn't gotten the memo.

Chase orders me a drink at the bar and I watch Alex, not far away, under an archway that's hand-painted with light-blue birds and cranberry-colored flowers. He stands tall, while the man with the pink tie leans against the wall.

They're in a circle talking to a woman who's facing me. She must be close to six feet. I watch as she smiles, her teeth big and white as squares in a Mondrian masterpiece.

I move closer to them while Chase is busy at the bar. A brunette joins their circle. It's evident that this woman will not crack a smile, and it amazes me how each of them tries to engage her in conversation. They attempt eye contact. They make jokes. The man with the pink leather tie rests a hand on her shoulder. Still, she never smiles, and people expend a lot of energy on the one single person in a room not smiling. I'm not talking about the downer. I'm talking about the one with the *you can't touch me* attitude, the one making a big fuss, too cool to participate. Self-importance has some kind of magical appeal, and people step up, as if dared, to get a non-smiler to part their cynical lips. It's like the world isn't right until they do.

I remind myself that the point of the evening is to sell Chase the Warhol. I need the money, so I stay close to him. Trying to form a bond, I bring up topics the rest of the crowd wouldn't know about. The Carpenters. Tom Jones. And Carole King. We talk about when Reagan was shot. And the television show *Dynasty*.

I sip vodka without a straw because I read that puckering creates fine lines around your lips. This is the reason I also gave up water bottles. Chase is talking, and I watch his mouth move, paying particular attention to his teeth, which are dark and ancient, and I have the urge to tell him about whitening strips. I want to tell him about Jasmine, too, and that we—he and I—are outdated, on our way to extinction. But I don't. Instead I make jokes, and keep things light. I need another drink so I order one from a server walking by with black caviar and crackers on a sterling tray.

"Your shoelace is untied," I say to Chase, pointing with my chin.

He hands me his scotch and props his foot onto a black velvet ottoman. Bending over to tie his shoe, he tries to act nimble as if this is no big deal, but I can tell he's struggling. He stands erect, straightens his tie, and smooths his designer jacket, in no rush at all.

"Don't worry. Take your time," I say, gesturing that I have both his drink and mine. "I've been used before."

Chase laughs and says he likes my self-deprecating humor. And I tell him I don't know what he's talking about. Throughout our conversation, I keep an eye on Alex and the man with the pink tie. Something's wrong. Something's different. And there's no way I can ask Alex about it. We have an unspoken contract, me and Alex. Not only at work, but in the bedroom, too. From the beginning, I made things easy. Too easy. No-strings-attached Kelly. Needless, wantless Kelly. A fraud, like art forgery.

Chase leads me to a wood-paneled den and shows me a Banksy. A balloon, a heart, a little girl. And I'm not exactly sure why, but I feel like crying.

"Are you OK?" Chase asks.

"I'm great. Thanks," I say, clinking my glass against his. We head back to the living room and join the party. A photographer waves a hand, motioning for Chase and me to get together. I hate having my picture taken in general, but especially on this day, with a glaring bruise and a reduced smile—I'm not in the mood. But Chase doesn't notice, or possibly he just doesn't care. He takes my hand, pulling me in. He drapes his arm around my

body in that gray-zone area—someplace in between am-
biguity and discomfort.

The photographer snaps a couple of pictures, and for
press reasons, I try my best to smile. Alex joins us and
more pictures are taken.

"She's a keeper," Chase tells Alex.

IN the cab on the way to Alex's apartment, we don't talk.
Not a single word. Alex is mad because Chase wants more
time to consider the Warhol. At the party, he said he
wanted "to live with her for a while." He actually said *her*
instead of *it*, and it bugged me so I gave him a mini-lec-
ture on patriarchy and art. Alex tried to make a joke out
of my little rant, reminding me I wasn't an NYU art his-
tory professor, but I wouldn't shut up. I went on, pontifi-
cating, and made the point somewhere in my monologue
that women are not property. I was drunk, but nobody
ever wants to be reprimanded, especially a man like
Chase. I tried to smooth things over after, flirting and
telling Chase I was kidding, but the damage was done.

In the elevator, Alex is texting and looking down. His
shoulder-length hair shields his face, and the silence is
deadening. I watch the numbers on the panel light up.
The ride seems to go on forever, and I'm just waiting for
it to end.

Alex opens his apartment door, and I'm transported.
Immediately there's this feeling that I'm in a magical, sa-
cred space. His apartment is full of treasures, works of art
that will get better with age like fine wine and cheese,
and I take pride in the fact that I know more about Alex's
art collection than he does. I discovered the artists, nego-

tiated the deals, sent the checks, arranged delivery, and supervised installation. Each piece is worth ten times more than I could make in a year.

Before I came along, Alex collected the old masters, but I encouraged him to acquire less-known works. To a civilian, the pieces have no value, they're like words of wisdom on deaf ears. Only an insider understands the significance of a fish tank with black sand and coral rock, housing swimming helmet crabs—performance art—or the human-size crayons stacked in a corner, or the pure white canvas with a black X painted through its center like a warning.

Jasmine pops into my mind, and I smirk, thinking of her lipstick-lined holster, but she disappears like a puff of smoke as soon as Alex touches me. I know he's still upset, and it's typical that he doesn't say what's on his mind, but I don't say anything either. I pour us more drinks, and we go to his bedroom.

I can't relax during sex. I keep checking on Alex. His eyes are closed, sealed shut. He won't look at me. *Open your eyes, Alex. Open them. Open sesame.* But he won't.

I need to shut him out, so I close my eyes too, and find myself considering who I am to Alex. And I come up with this list:

I'm convenient.

I'm smiley. (Or at least I used to be.)

We have sex following every date.

After, I always, every time, go back to my studio apart-ment in Chelsea.

Flawless, right?

As if I can turn away from the truth, I turn my head toward the painting on his bedroom wall, Roy Lichtenstein's *Drowning Girl, 1963.* I'm looking for eye contact, but her eyes are closed, too.

Before I know it, we're done, and I'm heading to the bathroom with a sheet draped around me, thinking about how I used to strut around Alex's apartment naked. I never imagined getting old. Nobody does.

I stand in the bathroom doorway. "Catch," I say, throwing him a warm, wet towel.

He wipes himself clean. "You know," he says, "tomorrow's a big day. Maybe it's best if you don't stay."

"OK," I say, as if this was ever a consideration.

"I'll get you an Uber," he says. And then he walks out of the room.

I sit up against Alex's white pillows, and catch a glimpse of myself in the dark-wood mirror leaning against his wall. The mascara Jasmine applied hours ago is smudged under my eyes, and the bruise near my mouth is deeper, darker than it was earlier in the evening.

I kick the soft, soft sheets off my body and get dressed. I dump the contents of my black velvet clutch onto Alex's bed, and push aside my reading glasses, the glasses Alex has never, not once, seen me wear. I rummage through my belongings like a madwoman: cell phone, twenty-dollar bill, ID, American Express card, Bloomingdale's receipt. Hidden amongst the lipstick, mascara, and concealer I bought from Jasmine, I find what I'm looking for.

I walk over to *Drowning Girl* with the tiny silver safety pin held high. I don't hesitate. I prick her right between her eyes. The damage is indiscernible to the naked eye, but under blacklight, the flaw will show. I put my belongings back, tuck my clutch under my arm and head home.

ACKNOWLEDGMENTS

Thank you, Dad, for tucking me in at night and captivating me with the magic of storytelling.

Thank you, Mom, an avid tennis player, for teaching me that you don't have to have the best forehand or the strongest backhand, you just have to get the ball over the net one more time. Patience, perseverance, and the long game were key in bringing this book to fruition.

Thank you, Susie Sutton, a dedicated teacher and careful reader who believed in me, and my writing, from the beginning. You read my first short story, and in true Pollyanna form, raved, but also, with subtlety and kindness, pointed out where I could've done things better. Your generosity and support are so appreciated.

Thank you, Alison Espach, a brilliant writing teacher and author, for your encouragement and insightful comments. Often you knew what I was trying to say before I did.

A special shout-out to all my brave She Writes Press sisters, and a heartfelt thank you to Brooke Warner, Lauren Wise, Crystal Patriarche, and the entire She Writes team. I have infinite appreciation for your important, visionary work and for the way you make dreams come true.

Thank you to the editors of the literary journals where these stories appeared. Much gratitude for your acceptances and for giving my stories a home.

A huge thank you to all my writing teachers throughout the years: Dani Shapiro, Antonya Nelson, Amy Bloom, Joan Silber, Tom Jenks, Susan Breen, Ellen Sussman, and Julie Regan (wherever you are). I so appreciate what each of you offered.

Thank you to my children: Jack, Richard, Rachel, Michael, and Elaine. Besides the fact that you've been my cheerleaders, social media advisors, computer tutors, editors, and first readers, you've brightened my heart and make each and every day a joy.

And finally, thank you to my husband, Mark, for listening to me read aloud when I needed an ear and for laughing in all the right places. Thank you for supporting my traveling to Bread Loaf and other writing conferences when it meant you'd be left at home with our five kids. And thank you for your patience all those Sundays when you found me still in my gray robe, writing, at two p.m.

ABOUT THE AUTHOR

CORIE ADJMI grew up in New Orleans. She started writing in her thirties, and her award-winning fiction and personal essays have appeared in over two dozen publications, including *North American Review, Indiana Review, South Dakota Review,* and more recently, HuffPost and Man Repeller. In 2019, *Life and Other Shortcomings* was a finalist for the G. S. Sharat Chandra Prize for short fiction from BkMk Press. When she is not writing, Corie does volunteer work, cooks, draws, bikes, and hikes. She and her husband have five children and a number of grandchildren, with more on the way. She lives and works in New York City.

SELECTED TITLES FROM SHE WRITES PRESS

She Writes Press is an independent publishing company founded to serve women writers everywhere. Visit us at www.shewritespress.com.

A Drop In The Ocean: A Novel by Jenni Ogden. $16.95, 978-1-63152-026-6. When middle-aged Anna Fergusson's research lab is abruptly closed, she flees Boston to an island on Australia's Great Barrier Reef—where, amongst the seabirds, nesting turtles, and eccentric islanders, she finds a family and learns some bittersweet lessons about love.

Magic Flute by Patricia Minger. $16.95, 978-1-63152-093-8. When a car accident puts an end to ambitious flutist Liz Morgan's dreams, she returns to her childhood hometown in Wales in an effort to reinvent her path.

Cleans Up Nicely by Linda Dahl. $16.95, 978-1-938314-38-4. The story of one gifted young woman's path from self-destruction to self-knowledge, set in mid-1970s Manhattan.

Again and Again by Ellen Bravo. $16.95, 978-1-63152-939-9. When the man who raped her roommate in college becomes a Senate candidate, women's rights leader Deborah Borenstein must make a choice—one that could determine control of the Senate, the course of a friendship, and the fate of a marriage.

Duck Pond Epiphany by Tracey Barnes Priestley. $16.95, 978-1-938314-24-7. When a mother of four delivers her last child to college, she has to decide what to do next—and her life takes a surprising turn.

Appetite by Sheila Grinell. $16.95, 978-1-63152-022-8. When twenty-five-year-old Jenn Adler brings home a guru fiancé from Bangalore, her parents must come to grips with the impending marriage—and its effect on their own relationship.